Alex Barr read *Mars as the Abode of Life* and wanted to be an astronomer, but Schrödinger's equation foxed him. His birth marked a turning point in the Battle of Britain and he wanted to be a pilot, but the RAF lost patience with him. After seven years as a journalist (reaching the zenith of his career as wire editor of *The Wichita Beacon*) he read *The Pleasures of Architecture* by Clough Williams-Ellis, gained a Dip. Arch. with Distinction from Portsmouth Polytechnic, and for seventeen years taught architecture at Manchester Met. In 1996 he and his wife Rosemarie (a ceramic artist) moved to a smallholding in north Pembrokeshire. His haphazard career has included work as a bus conductor, ice-cream vendor, kitchen porter, and garden labourer. He has won prizes for poems and short fiction, but none for sport. The stories in this collection span the period from 1980 to the present.

By the same author

Poetry:
Letting in the Carnival
Henry's Bridge
Orchards (translation)

For children:
Take a Look at Me-e-e!
Triangle Ted and the Grand TV Dance Competition
Jessica Vesica in the Land of Wedge Women
Penny Pentagon and the Hat Hunt
Rectangle Rex and His Pompous Pride
Lucy Lune and the Baby

MY LIFE WITH EVA

Alex Barr

PARTHIAN

Parthian, Cardigan SA43 1ED
www.parthianbooks.com
First published in 2017
© Alex Barr 2017
All Rights Reserved
ISBN 978-1-910901-98-4
Editor: Richard Davies
Typeset by Elaine Sharples
Printed by Lightning Source
Published with the financial support of the Welsh Books Council
British Library Cataloguing in Publication Data
A cataloguing record for this book is available from the British Library.

For Rosemarie
with love

Contents

Worthy

MacAllister's heart expanded and filled the enormous hall. It resonated with the organ music and the murmurs of graduating students. The stained glass windows full of saints and heraldry were all for him.

The graduands sat row on row. More were filing in, black gowns rustling. Soon they would receive, in yellow tubes, their scrolls. From his seat on the dais MacAllister sensed their pride and anticipation, though theirs were nothing to his. To one side of him were professors in a row like exotic birds, while behind and above, on a carved throne, sat the Vice-Chancellor. The organ played Strauss. MacAllister imagined waltzing with the beautiful Chinese girl in the front row. Perhaps later, inspired by his speech, she would congratulate him. Enter his gravitational field.

A thick-set man stopped by MacAllister's chair – the Bedellus. When MacAllister received his honorary doctorate, this man would hood him.

"I'm told this grand chair you're on was made by your father."

MacAllister smiled. "Indeed."

"You must feel pride."

"I do."

He thought of his father in collarless shirt and braces, bending to stoke the fire or sow peas in his allotment. Or reading to him:

Katie Bairdie had a coo
Black and white aboot the mou
Wasna that a denty coo?
Dance, Katie Bairdie.

He pictured the joinery shop, deep in aromatic shavings like angels' curls. Wee MacAllister bringing sandwiches.

"Ye brought ma piece? Guid wee laddie."

A broad smile on his father's chubby face. Reaching for the package, his broad hand briefly touched his son's. He took time to show the boy how to sharpen a chisel and cut a mortise. The sunlight caught every floating grain of dust. It lit this very chair, which was upside down. A peppery smell of oak as his father carved into the armrest.

"This chair's for the univairsity, son. And this wee birdie's my secret mark. A joiner needs his mark."

MacAllister felt under the armrest. There it was, the bird. The rough hollow of the figure contrasted with the smooth wood around. Now his heart filled the whole city, Govan to Shettleston, Pollokshaws to Bearsden. Yes, he thought, Glasgow belongs to me, not to mention Canada, the USA …

The Bedellus said suddenly, "I saw him just before he died."

"Sorry? Who?"

"Your father."

But the organ music changed and swelled. *Gaudeamus Igitur*! The Bedellus moved to his own seat, ready. The Professor of Contemporary Studies was moving to the mike, turning to grin at him, the sway of her heavy gown calling attention to the trimness of her ankles.

MacAllister had noticed the ankles an hour before, drinking sherry in her office. She was wearing purple tights and a short tweed skirt, and her bobbed hair was deep burgundy.

"You'll be voting yes to Independence," she remarked.

"Och, I may not vote. I'm used to the States now. Scotland's small."

"Small!"

"New York State alone has four times the population."

"And Scotland has ten times the history!"

He thought her mouth, shut tight in an accusing pout, would soften if he kissed it. That would show her. He thought the battle of wits had excited her. If she came on to him after the ceremony he might postpone his transatlantic flight.

"Vice-Chancellor," she announced into the mike, "I present to you Douglas Munro MacAllister, who has been found worthy to receive the honorary award of Doctor of Philosophy, for his sterling contribution to the international ..."

MacAllister's attention drifted. The Professor worked through his biography. Glasgow born and bred. Searched local pubs for talent. (Was she aware of the ambiguity?) Scoured the Western and Northern Isles. Set up recording studios and labels. Well-known names still obscure but for MacAllister. North America a rich field for his endeavours ...

He should have felt a glow of satisfaction. Instead he felt on edge. Someone must have opened the door to the antechamber, because there was a draught around his calves. It was June but the weather was dreadful. MacAllister pressed his legs together, trembling, and wound the black and crimson robes tighter.

'I saw him just before he died.' The phrase nagged him.

A light touch on his shoulder. It was the Bedellus, who moved away and beckoned, as if to say, 'Arise, MacAllister, stand before the Vice-Chancellor while he presents the scroll, and I place the hood in its parrot colours on your deserving shoulders.'

The Professor ended her oration, grinned at him again, and

3

resumed her seat. MacAllister stood. There was too much space and too much light and something was happening. Tide? Storm? No, a sea of applauding hands, pale or brown. The hanging lights below the great beams swayed a little. The stained glass reflected them.

Instead of approaching the Vice-Chancellor he spoke to the Bedellus.

"How long?"

"I beg your pardon?"

"How long before my father died did you see him?"

The Bedellus glanced towards the Vice-Chancellor, as if to excuse the delay. He said, "The day before. He said you were flying back and would be there any moment."

"I was too late!"

The Bedellus glanced again at the Vice-Chancellor, then anxiously at MacAllister.

"That's very sad, Mr MacAllister. At least you spent time with him in New York."

MacAllister closed his eyes. Like sea-mist rolling in to chill a warm beach, something invaded his heart. He surveyed the ocean of faces as if from a scaffold, then turned away. The Vice-Chancellor leaned forward to welcome him, smiling. His smile froze as MacAllister passed him and left the hall, down the oak stairs he had ascended in what seemed a different life. Through the ornate antechamber where he had been robed, down a stone spiral stair into numbing rain, the void of the Gothic courtyard.

"What's going on?"

The Professor and the Bedellus were standing over him.

"If you're sick, Mr MacAllister," said the Bedellus, "there nae use crouching here." MacAllister rose and confronted them. The Professor took off her glasses to wipe away the rain and he saw she had a cast in the left eye. He shrugged off his heavy gown and threw it aside. The Bedellus picked it off the flagstones, tutting.

"*Are* you ill, Douglas?" the Professor asked. "For heaven's sake, man, let us help."

"*Bodach bochd*," MacAllister said, and laughed. His laughter echoed harshly off the hallowed stonework.

"What?"

"You don't know the Gaelic? Poor old man."

They led him as if blind to shelter at the foot of the stone stair.

"Tell the VC he's recovering," the Professor told the Bedellus, "and will return in a moment."

"Aye, I will."

He sat on the lowest stair and the stone chilled him. The Professor stood close. MacAllister thought of parting her gown, leaning his head against her warm tweed belly and holding her warm purple thighs.

She tugged at her hair. "We need to go back."

"To the Taft Hotel?"

"The Taft … ? You're not making sense, Douglas."

"There's no going back ten years."

A picture of the hotel lobby flooded his mind. Manhattan traffic creeping by outside. His father, grey with exhaustion, rising from a soft armchair.

"Ye said there'd be a room for me, son."

"Jesus, Dad, when did you arrive? I'm so sorry, I've had meetings all day."

"Aye. If I could just get ma heid doon."

In the morning his father was snoring on the spare bed in his suite. He left a note. *See you for lunch, hopefully*. But he wasn't back till six. His father was in the room.

"More meetings, son?"

"I'm so sorry, Dad. I couldn't get away."

5

He couldn't get away from Judith García. They had the mastering done by midday and could have parted then, but no, he wanted her, though after many highballs the memory of his afternoon with her was a blur. The taxi back to the Taft seemed to take forever.

"Have you eaten, Dad? Let's go eat."

His father's burger was barely nibbled.

MacAllister sighed. "Tomorrow I'll cancel my appointments."

"My flight leaves at seven the morn."

"Oh no."

He ordered double Scotches. His father sipped his dutifully.

"They've given me six weeks."

"What do you mean?"

"Six weeks is what they've given me, son. I'm sorry."

"Oh my God."

His father smiled.

"I brought ye this."

Now on the cold steps, MacAllister remembered the texture of the wax-paper wrapping. The smoothness of the bowl inside, the scent of Tung oil.

"It's cherrywood, son. Turn it over."

The bird was incised in the base.

A few weeks later he was back in Glasgow. His father lay on a trolley in a cold basement. They had closed his eyes but his mouth was open, as if the Dark Angel had astonished him.

"Did he say a word about me before … ?"

"Aye, Mr MacAllister. 'Wee Douggie's flying in frae Canada. Be here ony moment.'"

As for the bowl, somewhere – Toronto, L.A., Vancouver, Orkney, Skye? – it was lost.

The Professor was looking at her watch. He studied her blue patent leather toes and the stone paving. A yellow snail was progressing.

"I'll announce you've been taken ill," she said.

Her heels clacked on the stair.

The rain ceased. The film of water on the courtyard shone. A small motherly woman arrived, breathless, with an Eastern look, in some kind of uniform.

"Sorry I late. I come to see, you need treatment."

He stood. She took his arm gently.

"Come."

"No."

He detached himself and started up the stairs. The woman ascended beside him in small bursts, comically.

The hall was full of space. The faces were a frozen tide. A different professor was speaking. *His* professor stood, and put her hand on his arm. The Bedellus restored his gown. The man at the mike announced, "But I see our honoured guest is back," and gave way with a gracious gesture.

MacAllister paused, then announced, "I am Douglas Munro MacAllister, son of Robert Allan MacAllister, Joiner." He looked up at the great beams, but they were blurred. He said, in too loud a voice the mike distorted, "And no way worthy to receive this honour."

The silence that followed seemed endless. He felt a touch at his waist. The Professor turned the mike off.

"Douglas," she hissed, shaking him, "don't do this to me."

He stared at her. Her centre parting was grey where the dyed hair had grown. Her face was close and he smelt stale cigarette breath. He nodded and turned the mike back on.

"Not worthy for myself, that is. But on behalf of my father, who made that fine chair behind me and who steeped me in Scottish culture, I accept it."

The Professor led the applause. He received his scroll from the Vice Chancellor, who tapped his head and shook his hand.

"Well done, Dr MacAllister. I liked the human touch. All right now?"

"Fine."

The Bedellus hooded him and motioned him back to the chair, and the ceremony continued. The stream of graduands seemed endless. He fingered the bird under the armrest and longed to hold the cherrywood bowl again.

Suddenly it was time for his speech. An anticipatory hush. A shuffling of feet, amplified by the acoustics. MacAllister had meant to speak impromptu, inspired like a revivalist preacher. But he read from his notes mechanically, hardly looking up, like a policeman in court reading a statement. The Chinese girl, snug in her green hood, looked blank.

The occasion ended with champagne and strawberries in the cloisters, which were open both sides. A chill wind whipped through. The Professor approached with a fixed smile.

"So what was all that? I feel dumped on."

"If we go somewhere warmer I'll explain."

He stroked her shoulder and tried to imagine her bedroom. Heavy blankets tucked in tight like those of his childhood. She lifted her face towards him. He thought she meant to kiss him, but she whispered, "Fancy yourself an expert at soothing angry women?"

MacAllister shivered. Greeted by colleagues, the Professor drifted away.

He thought again of the cherrywood bowl and tried to remember his travels. Perhaps, if he sent enough inquiries … whatever it took. And perhaps he *would* vote. He parted his robes and felt inside his jacket. His heart was there. Very small, but still beating, and that was a start.

Homecoming

It was only the plants they had to leave. Everything else went into crates. Bernard screwed down the lids while Rosalind noted the contents in a jotter. Before they even thought of checking the time, a big blue and green van appeared. The transfer company, five minutes early. The crew made breath clouds through their scarves in the subzero cold. Lit by the bright Kansas sun the boxes with their shadows looked solid. In fifteen minutes everything they owned was loaded.

The furniture was staying to be collected. Voluntary repossession. Their furniture had always been on credit, successive waves of it. This was the last wave. Bernard wandered through the bright rooms saying goodbye to it: the combination bed head and shelves covered in soft vinyl, the bookcase with trim that looked like brass but was paper. He remembered the spring day they ordered it all, from Mr Green's on Hydraulic Avenue where even the parquet was painted green. He remembered the high they felt when they found that, even with the business faltering, they could still get credit. Those were the days.

Bernard's ex-partner Wayne arrived to drive them to the airport motel. It was cosy in the cab, the three of them wedged together, Wayne smelling of Dentyne. Rosalind looked behind, at the suitcases in the back of the pickup, out in the cold. She felt neat and clean, her feelings packaged.

Wayne pulled out onto Eighteenth and paused for a moment so they could look back. At the front room window were the big cut-out leaves of the philodendron she and Bernard got in a garage sale when they first arrived. On the sill were the saw-tooth leaves of the aloe their daughter Lesley brought them from Arizona. Rosalind and Bernard caught one another's eyes. They both pulled faces and raised their eyebrows.

"It doesn't have that reproachful look," said Rosalind, "like it always did when we left to go on holiday."

Bernard nodded. "I know what you mean."

Now it was just a container, a box they'd lived in, storm windows worn but neat, ready for the next owner. The frost on the porch rail glinted. Beyond, the swing seat moved in the icy wind, brilliantly sunlit. Bernard remembered all those summers, Lesley with bunches, in dungarees stroking a guinea-pig, or riding on his back pulling his ears. Lesley and Rosalind cross-legged on a blanket, laughing, racing to eat popsicles before they melted.

"Okay, folks?" Wayne asked.

"Okay," they said.

He drove away fast.

At the motel they dumped the suitcases onto ribbed concrete which someone had marked with a finger *PG '91*. They hugged in a circle.

"So long, old horse, old buddy," said Wayne. "So long, Roz, you fantastic lady. And if you get to Italy, hello to Lesley." He paused and looked at their faces. "Hell, I wish things had've worked out."

"Recession is … recession," said Bernard. He wanted to feel some pain, to prolong the moment, but there was just this dryness, and the biting cold. They released each other.

Rosalind said, "We came with five hundred pounds. We're leaving with five thousand dollars. It's not so bad."

Wayne smiled. "Guess you about kept up with inflation." They tried to fix his smile in their minds.

"Home," Bernard told himself. "Not abroad, home."

The big black taxi moved quietly through grey light. It was like being under the sea, Rosalind thought. The bare plane trees left a disturbing amount of sky. They didn't arch over to form a vault like the trees in their street in Kansas. The taxi turned onto the road where Terry lived.

"I know this road," Bernard told her, surprised. "I used to come this way to school. There were no trees then."

The taxi stopped. Rosalind peered out. So this was Manchester.

"I even remember this house," he said.

He'd walked past it day after day. First in new cap and blazer. Later, hoping to avoid the searching eyes of prefects, smoking Woodbines to calm exam nerves. This roof had been here then, with its lozenge pattern of lighter coloured slates. As well as this gable with scalloped barge-boards. Waiting years and years for his brother to buy it. But houses didn't wait, did they? Houses didn't know there was a future.

Terry opened the door. "Well."

He was shiny-bald. Rosalind hardly recognised him. But of course, she hadn't seen him since he married Jill, well before Gulf War I. Whereas Bernard had seen him a year before Gulf War II, at their father's funeral in Abergele. By that time he was thinning. He shook Bernard's hand crisply and briefly, a business handshake. When Rosalind hugged him hard he looked embarrassed.

"Come along in."

But there was a great deal in the way: wooden gate, iron gate, porch door, front door, hall furniture, living-room door. Their suitcases came to rest looking forlorn, Bernard thought, after the bumps and scrapes.

11

"So," said Terry, with a round Mancunian 'o'. He looked at them briefly, then at the room, as if trying to guess how it seemed to them.

"So here we are," said Bernard. "How's Jill, Terry?"

"Off on holiday."

Bernard and Rosalind sank into unfamiliar chairs while Terry made a pot of tea. A young woman in Lycra leggings with short blonde hair came in. An au pair, perhaps.

"Oh, hiya," she said, and rummaged in a pile of magazines. Rosalind suddenly recognised her profile. It was their niece Angela. She waited for her to find what she was looking for, then hug them and ask, 'What was it like in the States?'

"Well, see you." Angela went out with a mail order catalogue. It was Terry, when he brought the tea, who asked the question. Bernard and Rosalind looked at each another. Where could they start?

Rosalind began, "Different from here, for sure. I've already noticed several differences." She paused, about to begin the list, and was saying, "One is –" when Terry cut in.

"These madmen. These militias. Sounds like you got out just in time."

Rosalind looked puzzled. They didn't know any militia members. A fellow in Mulvane drove a Humvee, but he was a loner, unconnected.

"Of course," Terry grinned, "you were into uniforms, Bernard."

"What?"

"In your business."

"Not uniforms, Terry. Work wear. Contract hire of work wear."

Terry smiled broadly. "Do workers in the States really have

their name on their overalls? On a little embroidered badge with *Dave* or *Sue*?"

"Of course."

Terry's face turned pink with amusement. They realised he was laughing silently. He laughed for a long time. They joined in politely, briefly.

In return for two months' food and lodging, Bernard was to help Terry in his electrical repair business. That had been arranged by letter. 'Further ideas when you get here.' Bernard thought this referred to a possible partnership, but as days went by and they fell into a routine Terry seemed to feel no need for discussion. When he talked it was to complain about the council, the VAT, or customers with delusions about prices.

By the second week Bernard was agitated. The heavy wire screens on the windows made him feel caged. The radio channel Terry favoured played songs he'd known in his youth. It was as if for forty years nothing had happened. As if he'd never left Manchester.

"Terry," he said suddenly halfway through a slack morning. "This is your decision, okay? But if there's some way I can fit in permanently, into this organisation I mean, tell me."

Terry didn't look up and nod and say, "Sure, Bernard, I'll think about it." He just scowled at the rusted terminals on a solenoid he was fixing. "Shit," he said.

After a moment Bernard added, "If there's anything I can do."

"You name it," Terry said dully, still not looking up.

"So, the scenes of your youth," said Rosalind.

He was showing her the playground in his old primary

13

school. It was hard to believe so much had happened in that small hard space: feuds and alliances, fights and friendships, games of 'stag' and five-stones. Hard to believe that, apart from getting smaller, it hadn't changed. They leaned their elbows on the green railings that had once loomed above Bernard like the walls of Jericho.

They walked round to the chip shop where he'd first set eyes on his first girl-friend. The girl herself had married and taken a surname he didn't know. Amazing: it was still a chip shop with white cracked tiles and brown plastic vinegar-shakers. In a third of a century nothing had been lost – except a sense of anticipation.

Rosalind felt she couldn't breathe. So these urban crannies were Bernard and Terry's patrimony. She herself had been brought up on different farms all over the South, with aunts and uncles, while her parents built and sold – or tried to sell – pipe organs to fairgrounds. She'd spun round in sunlit fields of barley-stubble till she fell down. She loved the dizziness, the confusion of up and down, the way the earth fitted against her back as if she were the one supporting it.

"Show me the hills," she said. "A stone circle if there is one."

She'd met and married Bernard in Southampton. Till now, all she'd seen of the North was Terry and Jill's wedding in Wilmslow. They hired a car, even though they thought it an extravagance, and set out for Arbor Low. They drove down the A6 through Stockport. In Hazel Grove they came to a standstill, then crawled at slower than walking pace. Bernard beat his hands on the wheel.

"Goddamn! What's all this traffic? What's happening today?"

"Maybe it's always this bad."

"You could drive to the hills in half an hour. What's gone wrong?"

"Relax, Bernie, there's no hurry."

But the tiny car oppressed him. The traffic was packed impossibly tight, the lanes were too narrow. The truck in his mirror was too close. Each time the traffic ahead moved on a yard or two, it roared impatiently and jerked forward. Bernard began to delay moving on, leaving a long gap ahead. The truck hooted. Bernard left even longer gaps. The truck pulled sharply into the inside lane, to aggrieved hooting from other traffic, and roared past.

"Did you see that?"

"Stay calm."

He drove on, steeling himself to the ridiculous fits and starts, holding back the things he wanted to say. He looked for a King's X or an Uncle John's where they could pull in and have coffee. Where they could look across a booth at each other, where he could say, "Who are these people, where are they all going? And why in cars? I thought in England people still walked or cycled." Where he could say, "I'm scared, Roz, what are we doing here? What am I doing with my life?" But there was nowhere like that here, only the odd small café straight onto the pavement, with no conceivable way of stopping outside. He was carried on in a slow tide of vehicles.

Out in the hills the road became dual carriageway. This was new. Bernard thought he recognised farms and hidden valleys he'd once seen at the mid-point of long walks, miles from a road. He slowed to look. It was hard to tell. He stopped. Traffic blared and swerved past him.

"Bastards!"

"I think that sign means don't stop."

It was an X in bleached-out red on a blue disc.

"It means Mac Fisheries," Bernard told her.

"What?"

"When I was a kid there was a Mac Fisheries in every high street. White X on a blue disc with four white fish."

"There are no fish on that one, Bernie."

"No, the seas have been trawled to death."

Rosalind looked at him coldly. "I want to go home."

"Home?"

"You know what I mean. Home is wherever I'm staying."

Bernard sat unable to move. She got out, went round, and opened the driver's door. Cars flashed and hooted. She prodded him and he moved across automatically, as he did if he was half asleep when she came to bed.

Rosalind found work, making phone calls for a bank to explain a new savings scheme. The call centre had a thick atmosphere of anxiety and a fast turnover of staff, but it would do for now. Bernard stopped trying to discuss the future with Terry. He forced himself to go through the local paper, passing 'Brownies take to the stage' and 'Off-licence knife attack' to reach 'Business Opportunities'. There he read 'This is what you've been looking for'. The advert was signed *Ken*.

Ken lived in a brick duplex – no, Bernard corrected himself, a brick semi. He was small and intense, with liquid eyes and a goatee beard. Every surface was piled with papers. The phone kept ringing. Business seemed to be good.

"So you've been in the States? Useful experience."

Bernard couldn't pin down Ken's faint accent. Australia? Birmingham? He wondered what Wayne was doing right now. Maybe this very thing. The old partnership had compressed to the nugget *experience*, like a forest crushed into coal.

"Business is business, Bernard. Whether it's work clothes or these little critters." He handed Bernard a lump of metal.

"They go on fuel lines and save fuel. You can read all the science in this leaflet, but let me tell you, they work. Figures prove it."

Bernard hefted the thing and turned it over. It was stove-enamelled a nice daffodil yellow. He put it down and studied the papers. There were testimonials from well-known firms, saying how fast they'd recouped their capital investments. He could feel Ken's eyes on his face, trying to construe his thoughts.

"But people are so hard to convince," Ken went on. "Suspicious. That's the bugger of it. And I need good people."

Bernard picked the thing up again. It was solid, for sure.

"I need time to think."

"Of course you do, Bernard. You must feel unsettled, just back in the UK. Tell me, do Native Americans really hug trees when they feel unhappy, or is that an urban myth?"

Bernard stared. He thought of young Cherokees, shown round the firm on work experience. How dazed they'd looked, as if their souls were off visiting elsewhere. He thought of the sullen Navaho help in South-western diners.

"Never heard that, Ken."

"Well Bernard, maybe *you* should try it."

Bernard laughed. The laugh relaxed him. He drank the coffee Ken had made and suddenly felt fine. Maybe this unlikely product was okay. Ken seemed okay. It didn't matter about his Nowhere accent, that was just prejudice. Wherever he was from, he'd chosen Manchester. So it would be okay for Bernard and Rosalind to live here.

"So where would I hug a tree, Ken? Chorlton Park?"

Ken pulled a face. "Nowhere here, Bernard. Haven't you felt it?"

"Felt what?"

"That the energy is blocked."

Ken looked at him intently, eyebrows raised, as if to say 'Significant moment – trust being established.'

"So why do you live here?"

Bernard was aware that his voice was sharper and higher.

"Good place to do business. Fortunately I have a little retreat in Cornwall. I go when I can." A long pause. "Convinced yet?"

In the States Bernard would have said, "No Ken, I'm not." Now he just looked away and shrugged.

Rosalind said slowly, "Perhaps it was a mistake."

"What?"

"Coming here."

Bernard said angrily across the dining table, "How can you say that? You think we can just pack up and go somewhere else? Where? How do we decide where? Drive round the country like tourists? How long will our stash of money last at that rate?"

Rosalind looked outside. In front of the clouds a 747 strained upwards with a noise like an over-revved motor-bike. In the kitchen Terry, washing up, coughed. From Angela's room came a faint thump of music.

Bernard sighed. "We should have known it would be like this. We should have psyched ourselves up for it."

A pause.

"I wanted to see you in your old home," Rosalind said. "To catch some of that belonging second hand. It's what all my life I thought I'd missed. But maybe it isn't something real."

He didn't know whether she meant it or was just being provocative, advertising herself in some way. He thought about the playground again, and suddenly longed for the certainties of childhood. The girls who were mysterious and unsullied. The boys you could be angry with and wrestle, then friendly with again. The games of sheriffs and outlaws you never doubted were worthwhile.

"What do you mean?" he asked.

"Maybe there's no such thing as belonging any more."

"Why not?"

"Because …" She couldn't explain. Because of technology? Fashion? Pollution? Globalisation? No, there was something else underneath it all, something she couldn't get at. "Because everything is up for grabs."

"What does that mean, Roz? What the fuck does that mean?"

"Don't talk to me like that. It wasn't exactly what I meant." She thought, *There's no exploring together any more, no groping in the dark and finding a friendly hand.*

Bernard said, "Well if you can't say what you mean, shut up. And stop casting gloom. Over there you got away with casting gloom because people were so upbeat, but don't do it here, right?"

She looked through the window angrily. The sky was still ruled into lines with contrails. The sound of dishwashing had stopped, apart from a plate being moved carefully now and then.

He went on, "And stop saying it was a mistake to come here. I do belong. So —"

"For God's sake get off my back!" Now it was too late, anger was in her head like rods. "'Stop saying, stop saying.' If you hadn't kept saying 'stop saying' you might have heard my warnings, the business might not have failed."

A terrible silence. Not a plate to be heard. Angela's music repeated the same pleading phrase. Bernard picked up a mug to throw on the floor, then realised it wasn't his. And the floor was carpet, not ceramic tiles like they'd had in Kansas, so it wouldn't have smashed anyway.

He went to Angela's bedroom. The door was open, she was sitting on the bed reading *Hello!* magazine. He knocked and

19

walked in but she didn't hear him. When she saw him she jumped up and backed away. Her eyes slid all round the room. Bernard turned off the music.

"Will you lend me your bike?"

"What? I don't know."

"Just say yes or no, Angela."

"I suppose."

Which way? The Cathedral, perhaps, built on a rock outcrop, even though streets had risen around it and changed the topography. The day was damp and not cold, not like winter – or any other season. He cycled past Manchester City football ground. A huge new stand in some pale metal soaked up the pale grey of the sky.

The surrounding streets of terraced houses echoed with isolated shouts. Women with thin white legs hurried along with pushchairs, as if the street wasn't where they wanted to be. Young men laughed, clustered round cars, hands cupping cigarettes. Cars crawled by throbbing with music from open windows. Bernard had once walked down this street with his father, and an old woman had said, 'Here y'are love,' and given him a mint imperial.

He cycled on. Yes, it had changed – for the better, he decided. Roz was wrong – he still felt waves of anger against her – a place could change and you could still belong. This neighbourhood had been a backwater, now it was a miniature Bronx or South Central L.A. Richly diverse, and –

He was going to be killed. Then he wasn't. He was just half off his bike, his heart like ice, with the front of a car six inches away. It had shot out from a side road without warning and halted with a terrifying squeal.

He wrenched the bike sideways and came alongside the driver's door. His legs were trembling.

"Idiot! Jerk! Moron!"

A youngish man swore back at him in some strange rhythmical code of unrecognisable words. Bernard rode on. The exercise calmed him. But when he stopped at a red light it occurred to him that the man might not take all that lying down. And indeed two or three cars behind was the roar of a gunned engine.

The lights changed, he rode on slowly, apprehensively. Before he could look round he felt the slipstream as the car shot past a few inches from him. It squealed to a halt ahead, at an angle to the pavement. There was something appalling about that angle.

Bernard looked for an escape route. He saw a passage between backyards, paved with setts, littered with used nappies and plastic bags. He took it. Brick walls went by in a blur. The fear gave him a feeling of elation. *But this is my home,* he thought, *Manchester not L.A. This shouldn't happen.*

He shot across the next street, looking out for the car. No sign—but he could imagine it about to squeal round the corner, right down on its offside springs. He pedalled into the passage opposite, slowing, his legs tiring.

It was like the way he once walked to school. As a small child he thought Manchester was formed of passages, like Venice with its canals, the air heavy and thick with smells from breweries and old men's pipes. Number One Passage, Number Two Passage, all the way up (he thought then) to Number One Million Passage. They were the heart of everything he'd belonged to. What number was this one? He didn't dare slow to look. What number would he die in?

He came out onto another street, quiet, without traffic, and turned left. Then right onto Moss Lane East. A sign said Universities. So there were two now. And a new cycle route along the edge of Whitworth Park. He took it. He was safe.

21

Passing Oxford Road station he decided to take a train. He got on the one that was waiting, not bothering to see where it went. He stayed in the parcel van with the bike, peering out to see how much he remembered, but the scenery made no impression on his mind. His thoughts went in angry circles – the argument with Rosalind, the traffic jam in Hazel Grove, the failed business, the unknown future, Terry's blankness, the man who'd nearly killed him. When the conductor came he asked for the next station and got off.

It was Bramhall. It came back to him, as he passed through the village, how he used to cycle here in his youth, with friends. If he kept his gaze high, on the familiar roofscape, and ignored the brash new signs, he could imagine it unchanged. He took the road uphill towards Woodford, his thigh muscles tingling. The air smelt fresh, the wind was cold and bracing. The houses were neat behind well-kept hedges. It was all soft and green and muted, not hard and red and echoing like Manchester. *I could live here,* he thought. *To hell with Roz, she can take it or leave it.* He went over things she'd done, mistakes, omissions, to stoke his anger.

Where the road levelled out there were fields on his left. It was still almost countryside. Beyond the fence to his right, JCBs at work. A new housing estate, perhaps. That was a pity, he remembered that field full of barley. Or was it wheat? Roz would know – but damn her, it didn't matter. He turned right past cottages, nurseries, market gardens. Memories came back. He and John Rose had parked their bikes by an oak and wandered through these fields, pulling at grasses, talking about girls they admired, about the future, what they were going to do with their lives. Perhaps the oak was still there – after all, they lived a thousand years.

It was.

It hung – seemed to hang – on the edge of an abyss. An enormous channel, a new kind of space.

The country lane was suspended over nothing. Aliens had loaded acres of greenhouse, wood, hedge, fence, and grass into a spaceship, and beamed in concrete to hold what was left together. Giant aliens, who lived at a different scale.

The new road marched east and west. Now Bernard saw that what he'd seen from the other lane wasn't housing. It was this road about to break through. Every path across fields had been severed like a nerve.

He wheeled the bike through the back gate of Terry's garden. It was a rectangle of coarse grass with one cherry tree and one mallow. As he shut the shed door on the bike Rosalind came down the five steps from the house and barred his way. Terry and Angela looked down from the kitchen window.

"Jill's gone," she said. "Left for good."

"Good God. Has Terry just told you?"

"No way. But he can't tell me where the atlas is, or the ironing board, or the Joni Mitchell albums. You don't take all that on holiday."

"Damn!"

"Why couldn't he tell us? Why?"

Rosalind scrutinised his face with a hurt expression. Bernard felt scoured clean by her gaze. He had no secrets from her, or at least, only the one, the big one he'd have to tell her now. Because holding back had made it seem not real. Like not going to the doctor, because once you went you admitted you were sick.

She looked into Bernard's eyes. They were alike, the two brothers, but one hadn't moved, hadn't changed from childhood, whereas this one, the one she'd helped to mould, for him there was hope.

He took her hands, steadying her as if to announce a death. "Listen."

"Go on."

He took deep breaths. "It's just … oh Jeez. This is awful."

"Bernard, come on."

He cried out, "It's a mistake. A terrible mistake, coming here. Oh God. I'm paralysed. I can't think. I can't imagine a new business. All I can think is places. Places, places, places. We don't belong anywhere, not anywhere on this earth."

Rosalind's eyes were wet. She kept her hands joined to his and pushed at him, wrestling him like an enemy. Terry and Angela continued watching as if it were a TV drama.

"I hate you," she said. "I hate you." She twisted his wrists, trying to hurt him. "For keeping everything hidden and putting me through hell before you crack. Then you're like a weed."

"This is awful," Bernard said. There it was again, the scrunching between his heart and stomach. Wrong, it had all gone wrong. "And the boxes haven't even come yet."

"Well that's good."

He stared at her. What did she mean? That now she'd go off like Jill, maybe live in Italy with Lesley? And he'd say, like Terry, 'Roz is on holiday.'

"You think it's good."

"We aren't slaves to that stuff. To a cause. Or even to one another." She was still trying to break his wrists and fingers. "Don't call it a mistake. Just say we trialled and errored."

He laughed. Rosalind laughed. In the steamed-up kitchen Terry and Angela rubbed at the glass.

She said, "Tried and erred. Wrong turning. Back to the junction, try again."

"Italy?" he murmured.

Rosalind shook her head. "Lesley would feel dumped on."

24

"We don't belong anywhere, Roz."

"We belong together."

Her words tumbled around in Bernard's mind, not making sense. 'I hate you.' 'We belong together.' Distracted, he forgot to push. She drove him back until he was against the brick garden wall. She was gritting her teeth, and beyond her wild hair the sky was a mass of contrails broadening into scarves of cloud. He thought, *I want clouds made by God, not man*, and angrily shoved her backwards. In the centre of the sour-looking grass she matched his strength again. Stalemate.

By now they were both in tears.

"All — those — partnerships," she gasped. Then after a deep breath, "Wayne — failed. Terry — failed. Look at him."

She sidestepped, turning them until Bernard saw the kitchen window framing Terry's blank white cipher of a face.

"Then Ken — no go," she muttered.

"I didn't quite trust him."

"You don't trust *me*. *I'm* your partner. *I* am."

Tears were streaming down her cheeks. The sad garden, the dark red bulk of the house, the dishonoured sky, froze like a painted backdrop, old and rumpled. Rosalind's face was new, as if he'd never seen it before. The play of feeling around her mouth and eyebrows. The way her eyes burned into him.

They heaved and heaved, and each felt the other's power, and the grip of the other's feet on the earth.

The Visitor

In a hospital bed in the north of England lies a very old woman. Her eyes are open and, yes, she's smiling, even though in a hundred and fifty days she's only had one visitor. Oh, there are chaplains and social workers and hospital radio DJs but they don't count. A visitor calls you 'Mother' or 'Gran' or 'Edie love', not plain Edith. A visitor brings you a magazine he or she hasn't read first, or a bottle of cordial, especially blackcurrant cordial. A visitor makes other patients nosy. Makes them glance across to see who it is and try to listen in to hear your secrets.

The ward is like any other — a smell of hot pipes and some sweetish chemical. With cheery handwritten notices, clusters of get-well cards, a lot of cream-coloured wall.

Edith is like many another very old woman, small with sunken eyes and a snow- white halo. When she isn't watching the doorway, the windowsill, or the gulls, she lies on her side and watches one of her neighbours. They come and go: back home, or to a larger building also called a home, or to a Chapel of Rest. Sometimes Edith whispers to herself, "Chapel of Rest, Chapel of Rest." It sounds like poetry.

The latest neighbour on her right is an old man. Yes, the rules are different here. In her youth she wasn't allowed to see a glowing young man in bed but an old one with parchment skin and bamboo legs, that's allowed now. Maybe it's supposed to be therapeutic. Another old man once got into this bed with her but only because he was confused. Her neighbour's immobilised by tubes. His name's Frank. Frank by name, Frank by nature he tells her every day in case she forgets. He also reminds her often how Sergeant Swann said, 'Pitch them tents down there, Corporal.' 'Not up there, Sarge?' 'No, down there.' And of course a flash flood carried the lot away.

Frank has regular visitors in different combinations. Some days a twosome, son and daughter-in-law, son and grandson, or daughter-in-law and grandson. Some days all three, other days just one, the son or the daughter-in-law. For some reason never just the grandson.

Afterwards, Frank says, "No visitors Edith?"

"No."

And he nods. Edith doesn't know what it means, the nod. But it's not surprising, visitors being in short supply. He does well to get three. Perhaps he thinks she should have played her cards right and stopped her children going abroad. But with him, Frank, to entertain her, who needs visitors? Now and then she feels he's being smug and that upsets her. Just one visitor, she thinks. One would be enough and enough is a feast.

The neighbour on her right is another small, very old woman. Her eyes are sunken even more than Edith's. Her halo of white is very tenuous. Like Frank, she's immobilised by tubes. She never speaks, just lies there, sometimes facing Edith, sometimes facing away. Her name is also Edith. It's written in marker pen on a square of plastic above her head. *Patient's Name: Edith Lowe.* Her name is also on a bottle on the locker beside her bed. Blackcurrant cordial brought by some great-nephew or grandson. At first, Edith eyed it with envy, then with resignation. Now with the get-well cards and the cream walls it's just part of the view.

The cordial remains unopened. Someone's written *Edith*

Lowe in marker on paper taped round the bottle but destiny doesn't mean it for Edith Lowe. At two o'clock one October morning, Edith is woken by a bustle and a swish of curtains. Her view is cut off by green material. Raised on one elbow she waits but the effort tires her and she falls asleep. In the morning, the curtains are open, the bed empty and stripped.

The cordial is still there on the locker. Edith squirms to the edge of the bed and reaches with both hands; she just manages to take hold. The crinkled foil at the top reminds her of Sunday School picnics. She moves it carefully across her body onto her own locker. She tries to tear off the label but her arthritic fingers won't manage that. She turns it so the label's away from Frank who when he wakes would feel called upon to comment. Ten minutes later, an auxiliary clears Edith Lowe's locker. Ten minutes later still, an old man is in the bed, unconscious.

Later, on her right, Frank's son arrives for a solo visit. He reads a sporting newspaper and every so often Frank asks a question. His son reads aloud some numbers or a name. At the foot of Edith's bed a figure appears. It's the ghost of Edith Lowe, wearing not a white shroud but a purple tracksuit. She has to be Edith Lowe because she has the same profile, the same flyaway eyebrows. She's been allowed to get younger, she's frowning, looking at the cordial. She's going to snatch it back to take for the angels. She's going to freeze Edith rigid with her Chapel of Rest eyes. The ghost pulls up a chair and takes Edith's hand. Edith flinches but the hand is warm. She's forgotten having your hand held by someone not in uniform.

"You look much better than I expected," says the ghost, who can't be a ghost of course, and must be a Chapel of Rest salesperson here to drum up business, disappointed to find Edith so perky.

"There's life in the old dog yet," Edith says.

The visitor asks, "Do you know who I am, Aunt Edie?"

Edith can still put two and two together. "My niece." Though really she has no niece.

"Great-niece. I'm not surprised you don't know me. I wouldn't have known you. It must be thirty years. I'm Annabel."

"Annabel!"

Edith smiles. A fake smile? No a real one. With her free hand she sandwiches Annabel's. She isn't to escape now. It's not every day you catch an Annabel. She turns to look at Frank who's staring across. Of course, this can't last. Any moment a nurse will say, 'Stop. Mistaken identity. Annabel: Chapel of Rest. Edith, give back that cordial.'

She'd better enjoy it now — but it's too late, Annabel is eyeing the white square above her head. *Patient's Name: Edith Edgar*. She glances back to the bottle marked *Edith Lowe*. She smiles. "I never knew your maiden name was Edgar."

"Ah," says Edith.

"Did you know that's what they've put?"

Edith shrugs.

Annabel says, "George told me you were in here. He said exactly where to find you — you know George. So I didn't even need to ask at the desk."

"I suppose it's a long way from ..."

"Dorchester, yes. I'm on my way to Dublin via Holyhead. I realised I could fit this in as a detour. I thought, How lovely to see Great-Aunt Edie again."

"Before she pops off?"

"That's right." They both laugh. Edith remembers her power to charm. Long forgotten, especially since Gerry died.

"Now, are they looking after you?" Annabel asks. "Are you getting all you need?"

"No. They aren't answering my questions." Mistake.

30

Annabel looks round; the doctor's in the doorway. She's going to get up and ask her sharply about Edith's progress. 'Edith Lowe? Chapel of Rest,' the doctor will say.

Annabel's hand is sliding, sliding away. Edith clutches with all her might.

"Not those questions. Why should I care what kills me or whether it takes another month or twelve?"

Annabel frowns, her eyes grow moist. Frank strains to hear. Edith beckons Annabel closer and speaks low. "They won't tell me what happens afterwards."

"Aunt Edie, that's a very big question."

"It is, isn't it?" Edith feels like a child praised by the teacher. She waits for Annabel to say more but Annabel's looking for inspiration among the big pipes below the ceiling. "I mean," Edith explains, "what's through the portal. *Is* there a portal, or are we just so much earth?"

Annabel looks vacant. She chews her bottom lip. "Have you spoken to the chaplain?"

"Yes. It's like being sold insurance."

Annabel grins. "You're a cynic. When I get home I'll tell everyone, Aunt Edie's a cynic."

"No," says Edith, "I'm not. A chaplain only tells me what he's paid to, only explains one policy. I want to know everything that's on offer."

"I don't think everything *is* on offer," Annabel murmurs. "I mean, whatever actually happens it's not as if you choose it."

Silence falls. The visitor's hand feels limp. She's still chewing her lip. This visit isn't working, Annabel may as well go.

Edith says angrily, "Well if I end up baked as a tile on somebody's windowsill I just hope they keep me clean."

Annabel bursts out laughing. The whole ward turns to see

where the musical laughter comes from. The whole ward sees that Edith has a visitor. "You might come back as one of those gulls," Annabel says. "That would be fun, all that soaring." They look appreciatively into each other's faces.

"Squawking," says Edith.

"Nothing to think about," Annabel adds, "but food and mating. Especially mating."

They both laugh this time, then Edith grows solemn. "Tell me Annabel, ought I to …?"

"To what?"

"Prepare myself."

A pause.

"Yes," replies Annabel.

"But how?"

A longer pause.

"I don't think I know."

Edith withdraws her hands. Annabel gets up. "I have to leave you, Aunt Edie, still a long way to go." Edith doesn't look at her. Annabel moves away, then comes back. "I've just remembered a morning I spent with you."

"When?"

"I was four or five. You took me rowing on some river and said things I didn't understand. About not having to row all the time, watching the colour of the water, avoiding shallow bits — was that it?"

"My memory's bad," says Edith, "and now you've given me more to think about."

"Oh God, Aunt Edie, I wish I could get you away from all this machinery and stuff. Take you to Ireland with me, walk you along the shore, show you the clouds flying and changing."

"I'll try to imagine," Edith says.

They know they won't see each other again.

"Goodbye Aunt Edie."

"Goodbye Annabel."

Weeks later, Annabel will arrive home to hear Edith Lowe died peacefully in her sleep. It'll appear she was the last in the family to see her alive. She'll tell them she left her in excellent spirits.

The visitors have gone and the light has drained from the sky. From the other half of the ward comes the babble of TV.

"So, you had a visitor," says Frank.

"Yes, from Dorchester. Do you know it?"

Frank shakes his head.

"Were you never stationed there in the war?"

"Never."

"Well, never mind," says Edith. "Would you like some blackcurrant cordial? I could ask the nurse to pour some."

"Yes please," Frank says modestly.

Edith is sitting back waiting for the nurse and smiling.

The Ones No-one Wanted

"Need help?" Liz asks the student in the corner. The girl's long rust-red hair strays over her drawing board. She's reading a battered copy of *Jazz UK* which has a dusty footprint, as well as checking her phone. Taped to the concrete column behind her is a photo of The Shard.

She looks up. Her eyes are brown lakes in a desert of acne. What can eyes do there but weep, thinks Liz. The girl isn't weeping, just looking persecuted. Liz resists a desire to turn away. This is her first student, and there's no-one else in the studio. If Liz gives up she's a castaway among tilted planes of drawing-boards under cruel strip-lights.

"I'm Liz, the new part-time tutor. Don will have mentioned me."

The girl frowns and takes music plugs from her ears.

"Where's the rest of your group?" Liz asks.

The girl suddenly sits up on her stool so her head comes level with Liz's. She's wearing army boots, a long wool skirt, and a leather jacket.

"I've lost contact."

Liz thinks of bleeps from space dying in a NASA control room.

"So how will contact resume?"

She hears a sound behind her, and turns before the girl gathers her thoughts to answer. Another student has appeared, a small-boned boy her own height, with blue-black hair and a round face a delicate shade of caramel.

"Hello," she says.

"Hello, please tell me what we must do today."

His chubby features show the strain of trying not to show he's unhappy. Liz knows the expression, she's seen it in her mirror.

"Hasn't Don told you?"

The boy looks blank.

The girl says kindly, "Mr Mockridge."

The boy's face creases with effort, trying to remember all the things Mr Mockridge said.

"*He's* lost touch with *his* group," says the girl, in an accent Liz can't place. Derby? Leicester?

The boy looks at the two foreigners, then opens his sketchbook while they look on. Inside the cover is the project sheet. He rereads the aims, objectives, and submission dates, then begins to search through the sketchbook, as if his group has got in there like pressed flowers. An oil-pastel sketch makes Liz catch her breath. A study of a boat lily, bold and beautiful, an explosion of reds and greens and purples.

Hard footsteps come out of nowhere. The boy closes his sketchbook as Don strides in. Liz had almost forgotten what he looks like: pale blue watery eyes, pale red-gold beard, high noble balding brow.

Now aims and objectives will come to life.

He frowns. "Les?"

"Liz."

"Liz, of course, Liz." But he still looks puzzled.

She laughs. "I have got the right day?"

"Oh yes. Yes of course. It's just that they're all out on site. Damn, damn."

Something cold crawls through Liz's insides. She replays Jack's breakfast, the smear of egg she wiped off his chin with her finger before rushing him to the day nursery. More sharply than she meant to, she says, "These two have lost their groups."

"Yes."

She waits for him to say more but he doesn't. Ah, but of course. Sink or swim. They're adults now, have to interpret aims and objectives for themselves. After all, education (she remembers reading) is a system for creating failures.

Don looks preoccupied. He mutters, "Llangollen, damn," looking like a prophet and checking his watch. Liz winces at his pronunciation.

"What's happening in *Llangollen*?" she asks, correcting him.

Don flashes a grin and she remembers their first meeting.

"Been asked to pick up some stuff there."

"Stuff?"

"Left behind last week. First Year residential project." He chews his lower lip. "You could come."

"Wherever I'm useful. As long as I'm back by five."

Don looks at the students. "Mel? Ismail? Fancy a trip?"

It's exactly right: four of them, four seats. Yellow polypropylene shells bolted to black steel frames, two each side of the table. Liz beside Ismail faces Don. Mel beside Don faces Ismail. No-one can pull up a chair from another table, no-one from another table can borrow one of theirs. An expanse of quarry tiles slides into the distance, under the door with the sign *Canolfan Crefft*.

No-one's talking. Maybe Don has reduced them to silence like a Zen master, like Socrates. Fixed them with his watery blue eyes: 'But what d'you *mean* when you say a building doesn't fit in? Or is well-proportioned? When you parrot the saying "Less is more"?' Forced them to admit they haven't digested Architecture. Which is where I come in, thinks Liz. A dose of educational liver salts.

The figures on the Craft Centre shelves are mostly female —

mermaids and warriors in fake bronze with long upper lips, proud nipples, and vermicelli hair. Liz asks Ismail what he thinks of them.

"I cannot judge such work."

"Where are you from?"

"Malaysia."

"So do you have different aesthetic criteria?"

The way he looks at her she might have spoken Welsh. She focuses on Don for help, but of course, he's done the spadework, it's for her to rake the tilth and pull weeds. They're punch-drunk from his challenges. She wonders whether Ismail thinks *Canolfan Crefft* is just an unfamiliar word in English. Or is he amazed to find, in this Extremadura of Britain, a language with a different flavour?

She's about to ask, but he deliberately looks away. She withdraws the tentacles of her attention.

Mel asks Ismail, "Where'd you buy that pen?"

"KL."

He takes it from his shirt pocket and hands it to her. The tutors smile — ah youth, when drafting pens are a novelty. Mel studies it from between the curtains of her hair. She's opened her leather jacket, revealing a black cotton T-shirt on which, printed in silver ink, is a crude drawing of a winged potato. Under it, in Lucida Blackletter, the words:

Seeking love
Taking flight

Mel gives back the pen and turns to the figures on the shelves.

"They're semi-perfect," she says defiantly.

Liz smiles and nods. The students are free to like anything as long as they justify their choice.

"What exactly d'you mean by semi-perfect, Mel?"

At last, a discussion on aesthetics. Or the ghost of one, because Mel's reply stays locked behind her eyes. She blushes, blotchily. Don sighs. Maybe this is not the time.

"Well this beats Staff House," Don says.

"Yes?"

"A change from weak coffee and weak conversation."

Liz wonders about the rest of the staff. This morning she was keen to meet them. Their conversation's weak? But maybe they have kind eyes.

"What are we picking up, Don?"

"Tents. Boxes of magazines."

"Magazines?"

"The publishers send boxes of complimentaries. We hand them out on the week. A lot get left."

"Which?"

"The ones no-one wants."

Liz looks at Ismail and Mel. How many magazines did they want? Silence falls, because of course, at twenty past the hour angels pass.

She asks them, "What did you do on the week?"

They both look at Don.

He says, "Environmental interventions."

"What, exactly?"

Mel says, "We hung stuff in trees."

"Ah."

Liz's heart warms. She pictures brilliant artefacts high in oak trees, wedged in bright angles of sky defined by dark branches. Crimson masks, long feathered tubes, webs of blue nylon rope hung with sheet metal curlicues and painted peg-dolls. A celebration. She'll see what they did and it'll all make sense: the course, the current project, the way groups have formed.

No use being impatient, trying to plug into the year group

instantly. Especially after years out of touch raising Jack. Setting up little pine blocks and arches and round red columns for him to knock down, instead of selecting facing bricks and floor finishes. Reading *Johnnie's Little House* instead of *The Architectural Review*. Turning out letters to practices, 'Dear Sir/Madam, I am 27, and …' But now she has this work for one term, one day a week.

"Let's go," she says. "Let's see these interventions."

It seems the residential week was at a farm camp-site. In the barn loft Don, farting gently with effort, bundles up tents and passes them to Ismail, halfway up a ladder. Breasting each tent like a figurehead, Ismail retreats to ground level. He and Mel roll the tents carefully, tucking in guy ropes, and thrust them into the bags Liz holds like giant condoms. Liz carries them to the van. The smell of canvas, the bits of grass and manure, remind her of old summers, school camps, undercooked potatoes, watery cocoa, whispered secrets:

'Liz? What do you want to be?'

'An architect. And you, Megan?'

'Own a fleet of yellow rowing boats with names like *Taliesin* and *Baldur*.'

She goes back in. The barn is of random rubble, but the doorway is edged with red engineering bricks, beautifully laid. When she turns to look outside the field is a hump of green dissolving in a bright wash of rain.

They finish the tents. Don and Liz leave Mel and Ismail in the barn and look in a shed for the magazines. The cardboard boxes have sagged with damp, and when they lift them the magazines slide out like flatfish. Endlessly repeated, the cover picture of the Burj Khalifa tower in Dubai, the world's tallest.

"Bollocks to this," says Don.

He finds some plastic feed sacks and starts to bundle them

in. Liz watches, hypnotised. Words and words, pictures and pictures, on glossy paper, sliding into the white, brown-smeared sacks.

"What do we do with them?" Liz asks.

"Ditch them."

"Recycle them? Shall I get the students to help?"

Don laughs. "If you call it helping."

Liz wants to know about Mel, the texture of her days.

"Did she print that T-shirt herself?"

"Complete with smudges."

"But she did it. Does Ismail like her?"

Don laughs again, and fixes her with his blue eyes, slightly bloodshot.

"He doesn't mix. They don't, you know. How can they when they don't drink?"

When the sacks are loaded Don goes to tell the farmer they've finished. Liz finds the students silent in the barn. She asks Ismail to show her the interventions. She expects to be led outside, but he opens his portfolio, which it seems he carries everywhere, and takes out a photo album. He's filled it with different shots of the same subject: a ribbon of mown grass curving through a meadow.

"This is intervention."

"Good photographs. Is Ismail your surname or Christian name?"

Right away she blushes, because of course none of his four names are Christian. There they all are on her copy of the year list. Most of the names are in upper and lower-case, but the Malaysian names are all upper-case. Perhaps because they pay higher fees, thinks Liz. Ismail, it seems, is a middle name. He doesn't respond.

They stand in the barn doorway, watching the white sky. Mel removes her jacket and drapes it on one shoulder like a hussar. On her back, under another winged, many-eyed potato, is the rest of the poem:

You won't know me
Till you bite.

"Did you do this potato poem, Mel?"

"It's a currant bun," she murmurs, fixing her brown eyes on Liz significantly, drawing her into her world. Liz feels a slight panic, as if stuck alone with Mel on a desert island.

To change the subject she asks them both, "How d'you get on with Don?"

Now she'll hear how, in sharp discussions, the word *design* has been taken apart and put back together like Rubik's cube.

Ismail says in his precise, fruity voice, "Very critical."

"We get on his wick," adds Mel.

"You two?"

"Everyone. When he gives out a project, he looks as if we've all pissed our pants."

Liz is about to say, "Surely not, Mel," but Ismail snorts with laughter. He puts a hand over his mouth, trying to stop himself. He keeps it there, an expensive watch on his wrist, and says as if from a well or cistern, "I overhear what our head of department say to our course leader."

He pronounces *our* with two syllables. Liz is charmed.

"What did he say?"

"Only send staff to Llangollen who are not useful."

Liz frowns and tilts her head back, as if to say, 'No more.' But he made a passable attempt at Llangollen.

Silence again. They wait. Liz begins to get anxious. Will they set off in time? But Don strides back through the rain.

"Are we fit?" he asks.

He farts again, and coughs to disguise it. They hurry to the van and Don gets into the driving-seat. He looks puzzled when Liz stands at his window.

"What about the environmental interventions?"

Now she knows he's eager to get back she's less anxious about time. He gets out automatically, neither willing nor resentful, and strides up the field towards a gate. The others follow. Their shoes squish in the hollows. The grass by the gate has been churned to mud by cows. They cling to the thick round gateposts to get by.

In the middle of the next field is a big ash, a tangle of ancient branches. Liz looks up but sees no masks, no feathers, no bright metal. Don looks around his feet, no doubt for the mower track, but it seems to have grown over already.

"Here," says Mel.

She points to the trunk at head height. Liz looks closer. A rusty nail has been driven in, and hung from it by a screw of green wire is a piece of sheep bone. On it someone has written, in black marker pen, ORNAMENT IS CRIME. Ismail unpacks his camera with its bulky telephoto lens and records the vestigial artefact.

Round the other side of the trunk Liz discovers more. Bits of card, bone, and blue polythene, nailed up and scrawled on in marker pen. One reads LESS IS MORE. Someone has drawn a line through MORE and written A BORE. Someone else has crossed out the whole lot and scribbled LESS IS LESS. Liz remembers these well-worn apothegms from her own student days.

The rain starts up again, a complex flurry of sound high on the ash leaves. Native leaves and yet alien, trapping tiny wedges of sky. Big drops fall half-heartedly on their heads. Further out the rain dances among the cowpats, and lying open to the sky are some of the magazines no-one wants.

They retreat against the trunk for shelter, backs to the bark.

In a ring. Clockwise: Liz, Ismail, Mel, Don, Liz again. She wants to shout out, as she did as a child when the rain drummed on leaves.

Curtains

I remember — I *must* remember — walking east on Hamilton Terrace that afternoon. The sun threw my shadow slantwise on the pavement. On my right across the waterway a tanker was unloading into huge cylindrical storage tanks. On my left I passed side streets that sloped upwards, as if Milford Haven was San Francisco. A gorgeous mix of clouds — pale grey tufts, white pompoms edged with gold, dove-coloured bands tinged pink — lifted my spirits.

I walked on and just before the war memorial reached the block with the café. I hadn't known what to expect, but I was satisfied. Pine chairs, plain green tablecloths, classical music (naturally) at low volume. A Polish girl brought me tea. No sign of the proprietress. Whatever happened, Harvey, I felt safe.

I sat with a view of the estuary, the stern of the tanker just in view. I thought about my last conversation with you. I was about to leave when a soft voice startled me.

"Waiting for your boat to come in?"

A small woman, full-bosomed, with crow's feet at her eyes and a red mouth pursed with amusement, was standing next to me. Not looking quite like the woman I'd expected, but still …

I said, "I'd like to see a tall three-master."

"A dreamer! Maybe those tanks over there are full of dreams, not oil."

She had a faraway look. I thought her remark silly, but liked her plain linen apron, free of slogans. Then she was gone and I paid the Polish girl. A hint of her perfume lingered.

'The sweet smell of the pure life' you called it. Thin smoke from the incense curled upwards lazily.

"So you'd like to be an *arahat*," you said, grinning, your teeth very white against your beard.

"A what?"

"A being who has escaped the endless cycle of suffering. Keen to try? The first step may be the hardest."

"Bring it on," I said. "I see suffering daily in my work. People who lose everything trying to prove their innocence. People who seem to age twenty years waiting for trial. I can't detach from it all."

You nodded. "You desire equanimity."

"Yes!"

I remember how your stroked your beard and looked at the ceiling. "Desire is a funny thing, David. It's at the root of suffering — you want what you haven't got, you want rid of something nasty — so desire must be overcome. But paradoxically, only desire drives you to overcome it."

We both laughed. I said, "I have that desire. I *will* overcome."

"Good. We'll do meditation together, then I'll chant a blessing."

How long ago that seems.

The energy from that conversation carried over into work.

"So you'd like to be a partner," Jane murmured.

"Should I have waited to be asked?"

"No, no. It may well be time. You've almost proved yourself. However, one last hurdle."

"Go on."

She pulled out three fat files and dropped them on her desk with a bang. "Three cases, David. Bloody awkward cases with irritating defendants. Wife-beater in Roch. Hit and run in

Pembroke Dock. Drug smuggling trawlermen in Milford Haven. Take your pick."

I know I have to remember this, Harvey. As if my mind didn't enter into it, my hand moved towards Milford.

I'm trying to remember the morning Carys was in the shower singing *Calon Lân*. After the *arahat* conversation with you, I think, but before the conversation with Jane. I was listening to a Bach cantata on my new laptop, feeling guilty in case I was too attached to the excellent sound quality.

Carys in a bathrobe leaned over me, smelling of Moroccan oil. The rich dark smell seemed at odds with her pale skin and fair hair.

"We sang that cantata," she said, an edge to her voice. "You should have come."

I sighed. "You know I dislike concerts. They usually start late, my back never fits the seat, and I'm stuck trying to be polite to people I hardly know." I turned off the music. "Forgive me?"

"I might," said Carys, and kissed my cheek.

The letterbox clattered. Carys collected the local paper, beaming.

"We're in," she said. The lead story was 'Choir's Festival Success', with a photograph of three rows of smiling faces, Carys at the front.

"Well done," I said, and gave her a squeeze.

I studied the faces, wondering what drove them. Did they sing to soothe some dissatisfaction, or to add one more charm to a bracelet of delights? I felt irritated with their smug expressions, so unlike their wide eyes and urgent mouths when singing. But I remembered your teaching about loving-kindness, Harvey, and tried to overcome the feeling.

In the front row a small woman lifted her face like a young bird to be fed. As if appealing to hear words of wisdom. If

Carys was a slender herbaceous plant, this woman was a succulent, firm and fleshy. Dark hair in some unfamiliar style. Feet together like a child on her best behaviour. I thought the words of a cantata would go straight to her heart.

"Which are soloists?" I asked.

"Him. Him. Her. Her. Me, obviously. And if I get my way, Martha soon will be." Her slim finger with its pink nail lighted on the bird-woman's face. "I'd ask her and Ted to dinner, but Ted has this thing with other men. Has to dominate them, and if he fails he sulks. And you'd go all prickly."

"And what do they do to earn a crust?"

"He's an estate agent, she runs a café in Milford Haven."

I'm trying to remember how I felt, Harvey. I think I envied Carys the satisfaction of helping someone become a soloist. Even though I knew envy is unskilful.

By the time I was ready for work she'd spread the table with books and essay notes.

"Yet another assignment on *War and Peace*, Carys?"

"This one's about Borodino."

"Remind me."

"The battle where Napoleon overreached himself."

I drove to work. I knew Carys needed the degree to get a better job, but I envied her the time. Yes, there it was again.

The defendants in the smuggling case were out on bail, so I could have called them to the office. But I wanted a break from box files and law reports. I thought sea air and a change of scene would do me good. And it was interesting to stroll among boxes of fish, oddly-shaped warehouses, pungent smells. The trawlers, yachts in the marina, tankers at the oil jetties, all gave me a sense of adventure.

The wheelhouse of the *Rosie Gomer* smelt of damp wool and engine oil. I could understand why my clients found heroin more profitable than haddock. The skipper and his brother had big noses and droopy eyes. Probably not very clever, I thought.

"I done nothing," the skipper complained, "and yet here I am charged with conspiracy."

I took some details.

He groaned. "Johnny got us into this."

"Is that the young deckhand?" I consulted my notes. "John Carew?"

"That's him. Fancied himself as an entrepreneur and got into debt with villains. Not as clever as he thought, eh?"

The brother said, "Yeah, we tried to help him out of a tight corner. Realised too late what he'd brought aboard."

I decided to confront the boy another time. The interview took till four thirty, so it wasn't worth going back to the office. It was then I first went to the café. We've talked about 'investigation of states', haven't we, Harvey? I felt that's what I was doing. Comparing perceptions. The Martha of the photograph, Martha in the flesh. I felt secure in my insight.

I went back a few days later to interview the young deckhand. His eyes roamed the wheelhouse, avoiding mine. He had bad skin and lifeless hair.

I said, "I need the name of your contact."

"Contact adhesive," he said brightly.

"A name, John."

"Evo Stik."

"No. Your supplier."

"B and Q."

"Please! Be serious. If you reveal your contact it will help your case."

"My Dad used it to mend his case."

I gave up. Nonsense answers have always been a ploy to avoid incrimination. Afterwards I went to the café. I told myself my last encounter with Martha had been too brief for detailed observation. Yes, Harvey, I *told* myself. Or someone inside me told me. I thought it might be the voice of wisdom, the inner voice that says, 'Hold on, David, you're on the verge of anger, step back from it before you make things worse.' Because I knew it was so easy to make things worse and create more suffering. The same voice seemed to say, 'Yes, David, you're secure, by all means investigate.'

Even so I was unprepared for the jolt when I saw Martha. This time her hair was pinned up, exposing a smooth neck. The place was empty and it was she who brought my order.

"So what brings you to these parts?"

I smiled. "The long arm of the law."

"Ah. My son wants to join the police. I tell him, 'So do homework instead of Facebook.'"

I laughed.

She asked, "Have you got kids?"

"Two, just gone off to college."

"Are you strict, or lax?"

"I have no formula. I deal with what's in the moment."

"That's impressive. My friend in the choir has two that age. Says she and her husband haven't a clue how to treat them."

I shivered. For a moment I'd forgotten her friendship with Carys. The reminder startled me. Silence fell. Martha stayed where she was, close enough for me to feel heat from her body. I smelt sweat as well as perfume. I told myself—yes, that phrase again—I was unmoved by these physical effects. Martha was merely bones and sinews, blood and urine. So my mission was proceeding well. I could learn about her from a psychological distance.

She said, "So, the law. Investigating a crime?"

"I *am* conducting an investigation. But I can't divulge the details. *Sub judice*."

"Wow, Latin, it must be serious. I suppose you're undercover. Better not ask your name."

I laughed again. "Better not."

Maybe I should have been an actor not a lawyer. I began to enjoy the idea that I was a secret agent, as if in a film. I tried to stand back from this feeling, to become the Watcher, that part of us you said keeps things on an even keel. I tried to be mindful, Harvey.

And it wasn't investigating Martha that drove me back a third time. No, no, I had to inspect the shed where the contraband had been stored. That was the main reason, I decided. But of course, there was nothing to stop me calling at the café.

Martha seemed to expect me. She sat opposite and let the Polish girl bring us tea. Her dark brown eyes held mine with a candid look. It made such a change from the guardedness of colleagues and the evasiveness of criminal clients. She clearly had a need to pour out her feelings, and I was glad to listen. I had a reputation for being wise. Carys always told me so. It was fascinating to hear a different woman's needs, and see how her mind worked.

She said that, ironically for the wife of an estate agent, her house was in need of repair. She envied her friend in the choir, a better singer with a nice modern house, married to a man who was highly respected but sadly not a lover of concerts. I felt a warm trickle of satisfaction on hearing that.

Martha said Ted treated her well, but with other people he would sound forth about this and that, oblivious to stifled yawns. He took refuge from the decline in house sales by watching endless rugby on TV. As for her son and daughter, one moment they were all hers, then suddenly twice the size complaining she was interfering.

I was glad she was very much a wife and mother. That made her safely remote, on a high branch out of reach, so to speak. I could listen to her musical voice as if in a hide.

She said she did once see a tall three-master in the waterway, but it was fake, part of a film.

At home I studied Carys to see if her sixth sense had registered my café visits, but she was deep in study and showed no sign, and I had no desire to distract her with my thoughts.

But I did ask, "How's the choir?"

"Hard going. Mozart's Mass in C."

"If it's in C it's easy, surely?"

"Glad you think so."

She sucked the end of her pencil and smiled. I asked why.

"I think Martha may have an admirer."

I felt a shock through my body. Jealousy? Surely not, I was only observing the woman. If she fell in love I could note the difference. I felt a need to change the subject.

"You were telling me about Borodino."

"At the start of 1812, Napoleon dominated Europe. By the end of that winter he had destroyed one of the largest armies Europe had ever seen. By invading Russia."

"I thought he was a military genius."

"So did he, David. He hoped for a swift victory to bring the Tsar to heel, but that was the limit of his planning. Any other goal was poorly defined. He hardly had enough supplies for even a short campaign."

"And Borodino?"

"A frontal attack, not his usual style. Panicky, perhaps. He won, but with terrible losses."

"I'll leave you to your essay."

"Thanks."

The thought that Martha had an admirer intrigued me. I thought it would be interesting to note the change in her. Would she be excited, or mellow? Either way, I felt confident that I could be secure and detached in my observation. The Watcher would notice any slip into unskilful mind-states. Meditation had instilled the habit of mindfulness—that's what I told myself.

Martha was neither excited nor mellow but distracted, a state I hadn't foreseen. Perhaps she was in love with this admirer. I decided to approach the topic obliquely.

"How are your friends?"

"What? Which friends?"

"Whichever are uppermost in your mind."

"You make me sound like a bookcase." There was an edge to her voice I hadn't heard before. She was tearing pieces off a paper napkin. She said, "Uppermost, since you use the term, would be Carys. Know what she told me? The sopranos in the Mozart have a harder job than the altos. Do you know the Mass in C? What do you think?"

The topic made me uncomfortable. I shrugged. I had to change it.

"You said your house needs work doing. What exactly?"

She narrowed her eyes. "Why are you asking?"

I shrugged. "Just making conversation."

"You don't *make* conversation. It happens or it doesn't."

She was shredding another napkin. Gently I took it off her.

She said, "My house. Let's start with the window. The thing that's meant to hold it open, doesn't."

"The casement stay?"

"Ah, the power of knowing the word. The *casement stay* won't go down on its pins. On warm nights the window bangs in the breeze."

"It keeps you awake?"

"Yes."

"Both of you?"

"Just me."

There was a pause. A very long pause. I looked at the coffee-soaked sugar in the bottom of my cup. Listening to Martha, I hadn't stirred it in. I could sense dark eyes boring into my skull.

In a low voice she added, "The *casement stay* is very stiff. If only the pins went into the holes."

"Oh dear."

Another pause.

"Perhaps you could take a look."

Her face was flushed — but it was a warm day. The sun beat on the windows. I knew her home was nearby on The Rath, a dignified crescent overlooking the estuary. Interesting houses which might be worth seeing. In asking advice she was like others who appealed to my wisdom. I felt solid and self-contained. It would be rude to refuse.

In her house I fiddled with the front room window.

"That's not the one keeping me awake."

"Which one is?"

She led me upstairs. To the bathroom, a box room, or a bedroom? If a bedroom it wasn't a problem because I told myself she was just a combination of elements, subject to decay. I laughed gently to myself as we entered a room with a super-king-size bed on which was a frilly duvet with pink and white candy stripes. All very feminine, but not enough to unbalance me. I thought of the psalm: *I shall not be greatly moved.* I thought of Gandhi, who tested his resolve by sleeping between virgins. I know, Harvey, I know. But he said he could lie naked with naked women, however beautiful, without being sexually excited, and still progress towards God.

I went to the bay window and examined the stay.

"Come away from there." Martha's voice was so thick I

hardly recognised it. "What if the neighbours see you? 'That Martha, well! A man in her bedroom!'"

I moved away and looked at the William Morris wallpaper, sun-bleached in places, and an ill-composed painting of Cadair Idris. The room darkened. I turned and saw in Martha's hand a remote control. She had closed the curtains. I made a mental note to buy a remote for the curtains at home, and was turning to go out when Martha hissed, "Wait!"

"Who? When?"

Carys had seen a mark on my shoulder-blade. I twisted to look in the mirror: a faded heart in lipstick.

"That conference on the Terrorism Act in Cardiff." I was surprised by my quick inventiveness. Now I had been discovered I was a cause of suffering. I had created karma with bad results. But I thought Carys would suffer less if my misconduct had been distant.

I said, "It only happened once. I was lonely."

"Lonely for one weekend?" Her eyes bored into me. "Did you talk a lot?"

"Not much."

"So when you're lonely the cure isn't talking but mindless drunken sex. At least I hope you were drunk."

"Extremely."

Drunk with my own wisdom, I reflected.

"What was her name?"

I wondered whether I could still take back the lie.

"I'm not sure."

"Oh come on."

"Sara, I think."

After which Carys cried a lot. After a few days she said she thought she might forgive me. After a week, when she felt like sex with me again, she saw the ghost of the lipstick heart, still there despite several showers. She ran downstairs and swept the 'improving books' you gave me off the bookshelf.

"They didn't *improve* you, did they David? I thought you believed in mindfulness? I thought you thought drink clouds the mind? Did you have to check whether it's true?"

The night was hot, and even with the window open the bedroom was stifling. There were distant shouts and the revving of motor-bikes.

I walked the streets beside Carys in a state of tension, like someone expecting an attack. In the supermarket I checked each aisle like a spy before rounding the corner. Waiting outside the changing-rooms in dress shops, I hid my face with a newspaper. I jumped when the phone rang or my mobile buzzed with a message. I wanted to be invisible, like a flatfish on the sea-bed. Seeing nobody, *being* nobody. But I accepted this, because I knew I deserved it.

When choir resumed after the summer Carys said, "There must be something in the air."

"What do you mean?"

"You aren't the only one who's cheated."

"Why, who … ?"

"Martha. She had an encounter with some detective."

A hot tremor of jealousy ran through me. It took me without warning. Yes, Harvey, my mind, which had once been so clear, had become muddy. After a moment I realised who the 'detective' was.

"And?"

"Got what he wanted then ditched her. How like a man."

This is so painful, Harvey. Each word is like a cut. But I have to tell you how the car made a hailstorm of gravel as it slewed into the drive and stopped with a screech. Carys got out like an automaton and rushed past me into the house. Things began falling from a window. It was the window of my study. I almost laughed because it was so bizarre.

I tried to tell myself this was serious, this was dreadful, but something inside me had shut down. I saw my laptop upright in a flower bed like a drunken gravestone, and near it, in a drift of scattered clothing, the shirt Martha unbuttoned that afternoon on The Rath. Carys's silence was appalling, like the silence of someone drowning. There was nothing I could say. I picked up my laptop and the most vulnerable of my clothes and papers. I walked to the end of the road, called a taxi, and went to a hotel.

Carys divorced me as you know. I contested nothing. When I called on her to collect my things she studied me like a phrase in some unknown language. Her eyes were the colour of winter sky. She told me her so-called friend had left the choir.

Jane tapped the desk with her pencil, pursing her lips.

I said, "I'm trying to work out where it went wrong."

"You briefed John Carew's counsel to plead guilty. Despite the boy's severe learning disability and inability to read. You believed the false evidence from the skipper and his brother and assumed they were innocent. Fortunately counsel got the real picture in time. Entrepreneur indeed! John Carew can barely sign his name."

"I realise —"

"These are from Carmarthen branch." She made a fan of client files on the desk. "Where they'll give you an office. Delyth takes over criminal work here."

They were requests for will writing. I had slipped back twenty years.

Jane said, "Take your pick."

Harvey, you asked me to spot the point of no return. I've spent many lonely evenings wondering. Was it going up to the bedroom? Surely that was innocent curiosity. To see the different style of another couple's bedroom. Maybe the change in Martha's voice—'Come away from there!'—unbalanced me. But I was about to leave. What stopped me? Surely not Martha saying, 'Wait!'. Was the habit of obedience so strong? Or was it curiosity again? Because I couldn't think what she was about to say?

These investigations tire me. What are they supposed to teach? How to act on some unlikely future occasion? In my celibate life I find myself dwelling—oh yes, guiltily!—on the memory of that afternoon with Martha. When she took off her blouse, could I still have left? When she bared her breasts, wide eyes challenging me to touch her, could I have held back? Her smooth brown skin, her large dark areolas, were too much. Her bare arms gleamed in the half-light. Her skin was hot, with a film of sweat. Her eyes half closed with pleasure, her mouth opened as if to sing. It was a parallel universe. The world beyond the curtains was unreal. The scent of sweat and perfume undid me.

But into that memory another swirls its poison. A sunset with red-tinged cirrus. A car with a gash all along one side slewing into the drive. A study window spewing clothes, books, papers, laptop. And even the curtains on their pole, like the dishonoured standard of a beaten army.

At first nothing seemed real. But as the consequences piled up my perceptions sharpened. You said, 'The thing about the Path, David: the higher one gets, the harder the fall. I'm sending you on a course for beginners.' And you asked me for this report.

How One Thing Becomes Another

A train from Florence rumbles through the night heading for Paris. Dr Tanner watches the world slide by and thinks of his daughter. Will she like the Tuscan doll he bought? Is she too old for dolls at eleven? Seven years divorced, he's unsure about many things. But he is sure about the Italian Renaissance.

Right now he's reading about Orsanmichele, the church in Florence converted from a grain market. The book is in Italian.

"So you read Italian. Wish I did."

It's the woman opposite. Rounded features, clear eyes, a slight lift to her upper lip like Della Robbia's *Madonna of the Innocents*. But warm flesh, not cold terracotta, with lines of amusement around her mouth.

"Ah, you speak English."

She smiles. "I think we all do in this compartment. My husband does, after a fashion. And the gentleman beside you, judging from his newspaper."

That gentleman lowers his paper – one Tanner disapproves of – and grins. "All bloody Brits, eh? What a coincidence."

She shrugs. "I suppose we all booked on the same website."

Silence falls. No-one seems able to further the conversation. Tanner hands the book to the woman.

"Have a look."

"Thank you."

She turns the pages carefully, studying the photographs. The husband leans over, his weight on her shoulder.

"Buildings," he says.

She moves away from him. He struggles to stay upright against the swaying of the train. His cream-colored jacket is unbuttoned, revealing a purple T-shirt with the slogan *Don't ask me to sing*. He refills his plastic beaker with Barolo and drinks. His long nose and hollow cheeks remind Dr Tanner of Cosimo de' Medici.

"What do you do?" the woman asks.

Tanner wishes he did famine relief or mountaineering, something everyone could admire. He sighs. "I lecture in art history, specialising in the Renaissance."

"That must be fascinating."

"Yes, but there are occupational hazards."

"Good heavens. What?"

"It can make you very dry."

Cosimo's lookalike perks up and offers him the Barolo.

"Thank you," says Dr Tanner, "but it wouldn't agree with me."

"It agrees fine with me."

He laughs, spills wine on the seat, and wipes it with his sleeve.

The woman goes back to studying the book. Dr Tanner is struck by her interest. A refreshing change from vague or embittered colleagues. And students who mostly lack the spark of curiosity. It would be so rewarding to teach her Italian.

"What do *you* do?" he asks.

"Bugger all," her husband growls.

"I do plenty," his wife says. "For example, I organise fund-raising for —"

Her husband hiccups, spills more wine, and swears.

Another silence.

The man with the newspaper, fiftyish with a toothbrush

moustache, wearing a loose green cardigan over a yellow open-necked shirt, leans towards Dr Tanner.

"I do Italian. *Buona sera. Dolce vita.* Pizza *margherita.*"

When no-one responds he says to the woman, "Come on then, love, tell us about the book."

She indicates that the answer should come from Tanner.

He sighs again. "Orsanmichele was once a grain market. The upper floor was the granary. You can still see the ducts the grain came down."

"When did it become a church?" the woman asks.

"Around 1380."

"Why?"

"It seems there was a miracle."

The woman's husband belches.

The train sways on, the noise of wheels a reminder of the hard rails beneath. The swaying tips the husband against his wife, who pushes him upright. He opens his eyes with a start and gets to his feet, clutching the luggage rack.

"Going for a pee."

He slides open the compartment door and goes out. Tanner suppresses the thought, Good Riddance.

The man beside him asks, "What do you know about the Great Apennine Tunnel?"

Tanner says guardedly, "Nothing."

"One of the railway wonders of the world, on the line between Florence and Bolog-ner."

Tanner cringes at his pronunciation.

"Built under Mussolini," the man goes on. "The line from Rome to Milan used to wiggle over the mountains. The new route transformed the journey."

He sits back as if to say, 'So there.'

Silence again.

61

The woman returns Tanner's book with a smile.

"Interesting how one thing becomes another. Wish I'd seen those grain ducts."

"You must go back sometime."

She nods, then dozes. He tries to picture where she and her husband live. Maybe some grand Edwardian house in Sussex overlooking the sea. He imagines being a party guest there. He'd encourage the husband to sing … then laugh.

A frown puckers the woman's smooth forehead, as if some dream troubles her. She's wearing a knee-length dress in some soft material, simple but elegant. From the *Via Tornabuoni*? Or the *Via del Corso*? That was where he bought the doll, in desperation. Would chocolates have been better? Whichever he chose his ex-wife would comment on, not unkindly but nevertheless demeaning.

His daughter comes at weekends, often with a crowd of friends. Their conversation seems to be in code. But he feeds them all enthusiastically, to show how much he cares.

He too dozes. When he opens his eyes he senses a change. The train has stopped. When time passes and it fails to move the woman becomes restless and wakes.

"Any idea where we are?" she asks.

"Near Genoa, I imagine."

"Oh, isn't Genoa famous for pirates?"

"Aha, me hearties! Stand by to repel boarders," says the railway buff.

More silence.

Suddenly the compartment door slides open, but instead of the woman's husband it's a tall man in a leather jacket. His bulk seems to fill the space. He has Italian features but is holding a British passport.

To the woman he says, "Excuse I interrupt. *Signora* Price?"

"Yes, that's me."

"Excuse I must tell to you about your husband. He fall. From the train."

The pink roses in the woman's cheeks turn white in an instant.

"Oh God. Where is he?"

She makes to get up. The plainclothes policeman gestures to stay put.

"Please, *signora*. We tell to you when you should descend."

He goes out. The woman's eyes search the luggage racks, the curtains, the empty windows, as if for clues, then rest on Tanner's face.

"How could he fall? He only went to the toilet."

"Perhaps he mistook the train door for the toilet door. They are close."

"Oh God. Is he dead?"

Tanner's neighbour says, "We were doing eighty at least, love. He'll be scobbled."

A long silence. Tanner misses the reassuring noise of wheels, and feels ill at ease. The policeman was a disturbing presence, with his beard shadow and the smell of Paco Rabanne or whatever. And his bulk, like the detective-sergeant who stood over him in a guarded bedroom, at that student party where something had been stolen and drugs sold.

Dr Tanner remembers that long-ago conversation:

"Empty your pockets."

Fluff, a chocolate wrapper, condoms.

"On the pull, were we? Not much luck, eh, son? I see they're unopened. You'll have to pull yourself."

The detective laughed. Tanner tried to imagine himself as a waxwork melting onto the carpet. The interview wasn't over. The man was enjoying himself.

"Ribbed for extra satisfaction, eh? But is three enough for one night?"

And more of the same. The worst thing was the hatred welling up in him like bile.

The compartment suddenly seems confined. Darkness presses against the window. The wood veneer on the partition reminds him of the furniture of a boring aunt and uncle. The notices about not smoking or leaning out strip the language of Dante bare of charm. He looks at the woman and tries to think of something useful or soothing. But how does one soothe a woman about to identify the abraded corpse of her husband?

He makes eye contact with her with a rueful grimace. She makes a rueful grimace back. Tanner's neighbour looks from one to the other as if curious what either will do or say, and now and then sighs sympathetically.

The compartment door slides open again and a short stout Italian in a leather jacket comes in.

"*Signora* Price?"

Another policeman. Naturally there are two, posted on the train for just this kind of occasion.

"Shall I bring my luggage?"

"Excuse? I not good English."

Dr Tanner says, "*Volete che la signora porti fuori i suoi bagagli?*"

"*Ah, si, si.*"

The stout policeman beams. He explains in Italian that the lady should indeed bring her luggage and descend because the train must move on. Tanner translates this for the widow. She stands with a hunted look and goes to pull down two suitcases from the rack. He gets up to help, but the handles are the kind that tuck in flush with the body, and he can't get a grip. His hand and the woman's touch.

"It's okay," she says, "I'll do it."

He sits down again. The suitcases land with a thump in front of him.

"You'll need help, love," says Tanner's neighbour. "Our friend here will get off with you. Interpolate for you."

The widow glances briefly at her rescuer-elect, then away, her eyes losing focus. Through Tanner's mind impressions flit too quickly to deal with. Why 'our friend'? None of them even know one another's names. And the fellow made it sound like 'R. Friend' as if *that* was his name. And how irritating, 'interpolate' instead of 'interpret'. And it's late. Instead of dozing the night away in his seat he'd spend it on a hard chair in some echoing tiled police post, and he needs sleep because when he returns he needs to give his full attention to the contentious, if not libellous, email from Professor Kastner about the authenticity of the newly discovered Giotto drawings.

He pictures the husband's body, scraped bloodily raw, the Cosimo de' Medici profile flayed to the skull, the brain pan empty, and how he'd thought Good Riddance when the man lurched out to pee. How he'd ignored him, giving his wife all the attention, so the man felt unwanted and left the compartment. The police would pick up on that, his complicity in sending the husband to his death, because that was their job. The way they looked at you, you felt you must have done something wrong or would have a hell of a job to convince them that you hadn't.

The railway buff is looking at him, probably to say more about tunnels. A sudden longing seizes him. He should be living in the open air, in the mountains, with the plains far below. He imagines Kastner lost in a ravine, calling for help. Tanner would have his daughter with him. She'd help to throw Kastner a rope, because she's quite mature, and the doll *is* a bad idea but the sooner he gets back to Britain and arranges to see her the sooner he can put that embarrassment behind him. Then back to his books and lecture notes …

His neighbour is standing now and for some reason taking his own suitcase down from the rack.

"I'll get off with you, love," he says to the widow. "I do Italian."

But this is wrong. Tanner blinks. There's something in the situation he isn't quite getting hold of. He blinks and blinks, and suddenly the compartment is empty, the door still wide, and he rushes into the corridor and catches up with the woman, but the railway buff is already halfway down the carriage with the stout policeman, carrying his own case and one of the widow's, and it's too late to call them back.

He must have blurted out something because the widow turns to look at him.

"The book," he says. "Orsanmichele. Have it. Please."

"I think you need it more than I do."

She turns and moves along the corridor, obeying the laws of perspective.

After an interval the train moves on.

My Life with Eva

Lying here in our acres of scented summer grass, looking up at a million stars, I think how one wrong move in the past could have forfeited all this. As if I lost my way and turned north into frozen wastes instead of south into lush pasture. The stars are so clear because the nearest street light is a mile off, and the house (which in any case is unlit) is fifty paces away beyond the stream. There's only one glow, a gentle yellow almost lost in the warm night, where the roof light of Eva's studio confirms her presence. A radiance too muted to dilute the black of the heavens, as Eva herself never dilutes my dreams.

Faint sounds emerge from a background of silence. One is the stream whose music hovers around a few notes in a teasing indefinable rhythm. Another is the rustle of small birds in the hedgerow whose black outline cuts the sky when I tilt my head back. Which shows that although the zenith has drunk every ounce of light (apart from the stars themselves), the horizon is lighter, the deep purple of Eva's best silk dress. Further off is the scratching of some restless ewe cropping grass, not content to kneel like the rest of our flock. And further still, from the next smallholding, the faint anxious bark of our neighbours' dog. Ah yes, and there, almost too eerie and sudden to be real, an owl's cry. For a moment just now I imagined voices, which seems unlikely because Eva never carries the phone to her studio, and is working alone with her favorite samba music, sensual but too soft to carry far.

I deserve to lie here and rest my bones after a day spent cutting and uprooting brambles. My arms ache and in the crook of my elbow I can feel a sticking plaster, over a nasty scratch no doubt. It's good to think that Eva put it on me, wiping the wound and kissing it, while dressed in her white overalls with their pattern of scorch marks and dabs of tertiary color, which remind me of an old lab coat of my father's I inherited to paint in. Yes, I'm glad to lie here on this recliner among the tall feathery grasses, away from the blanking glare of streetlights, greeting Orion, the Plough, Cassiopeia, Leo, in their dance around the Pole Star, while the pale amber moon struggles to rise free from the hawthorn branches it's caught in, and the breeze brings the tobacco scent of hay from our open barn. And I remember lying on a beach in Greece when the dark sky had swallowed the dregs of daylight along the western sea horizon, watching the familiar constellations named by Greeks.

Who lay beside me then? Ah, it can only have been Eva, my philosophical, pragmatic fellow-backpacker Eva, unfazed even though we'd found no place to stay after taking the last bus to that xenophobic little fishing village where a stranger who spoke bad Greek was thought dangerous or mad. Unless I remember wrong, when the night breeze off the water began to chill us we rose and walked through the night, Eva's eyes in the moonlight shining with adventure, to the port where we caught the first boat off the island, humming the tune of *To karavi fevyi ta misonikhta* (I heard it again on YouTube years later) and laughing because it was well past *misonikhta*, midnight, when the boat left.

Any woman but Eva might have blamed my lack of foresight and sat head in hands moaning for a bed and supper. Who do I have in mind? Deirdre I suppose, dear little Deirdre (I was always fond of her) who would have insisted on the dreary conformity of package tours and hotel chains. Deirdre who if I'd married her would have kept me tied to that industrial town in the North of England. The town we grew up in, safe and sound and close to our parents and siblings, leading today to a rooted and respectable retirement. Instead of which I'm here with Eva near the western sea in this place visitors call remote and we call the hub of the universe. Where we created a garden from bare fields, grew much of our own food until old age crept over us, struggled to stop sheep and goats escaping and streams overflowing, built structures with our bare hands, and when snowed in for weeks relaxed in that hush of whiteness into companionable hibernation by the log-stove. Where we never felt isolated, under skies alive with buzzards, kites, crows, woodpeckers, starlings, sparrows (and in summer the swallows — ah, the swallows!) among fields populated with voles, badgers, foxes, butterflies, dragonflies … and of course our sheep, our goats, our cats, and our Welsh cob.

The bright heads of marigolds, campions, hellebores, scabious, heucheras, and schizostylis nod in the breeze as if to say, 'Yes, you did it, the two of you', and yet I sometimes fear the magic of the place, as if one day like Thomas the Rhymer, or that shepherd boy on the Preseli Hills, I might wake with starved lips on a bare hillside having offended my fairy hosts. Or wake to find Eva dead beside me, Eva the star that like a wise man I followed.

But nothing can take away the past, the travels we now rest from. They seemed at the time like adventures, though nowadays on TV smug comedians and presenters seem keen to retrace our steps and smear them with their bloated personalities. A recent series about the Inca Trail in Bolivia brought it back to us — the fireflies, the rope bridges across lush steep-sided valleys, the dark-skinned women with black hair in plaits, and the danger of being murdered by cocaine barons. I thought our wanderings in the less trodden parts of Venice were unusual, finding cheap hidden restaurants frequented by *vaporetto* drivers where Eva tried out phrases from Grand Opera. But no, my cousin Bill the Vivaldi devotee insists on covering the same ground, enthusing about 'canals that turn in on themselves endlessly like an Escher print'. Oh well. Our backpacking days are over, but there's plenty to look back on.

How strange to think that in my youth I was shy of Eva for months on end, overawed by her Cleopatra profile, her long waves of chestnut hair, her majestic proud-bosomed gait, and some perfume I never found the name of trailing her progress like unheard music. Too shy to ask her to dance (ballroom in those far-off days, waltzes and quicksteps, with the odd Veleta or Virginia reel) until one evening in the vestibule of that church hall we collided, drew back and stared at one another, and I, who never blurted, blurted, "I want to dance and dance and dance with you, Eva," and those grey eyes flashed very wide and her smile was a supernova. Nothing more needed saying, we were already linked at a deeper level, and when I took her in my arms and waltzed her around that formerly featureless but suddenly enchanted hall, nearly fainting with excitement as her thighs brushed mine, the encounter spelt doom for any other girl I had been going out with.

At the time of my first waltz with Eva my girlfriend was Deirdre, though 'companion' is a better word. We controlled 'defects of loneliness' in one another. We kissed, I felt her breasts through her jumper, and that was all — my grandchildren's generation would think that strange. But then the least contact between bodies was exciting — in the dance 'Hands, knees, and *bumps*-a daisy' for example, where we turned and bumped bottoms with our partners. Deirdre's bump was far from equal and opposite, so I nearly knocked her over, whereas Eva — ah, Eva! — connected with such a satisfying thump I could imagine the firm but yielding flesh of her whole body.

I remember Deirdre at those hops for young people as a round-faced ash-blonde girl sitting upright with hands neatly in her lap, looking up at me when I first asked her to dance as if surprised, and murmuring, "Oh. All right. Thank you." Whereas Eva often sat, if there was room, with her long legs propped on the neighbouring chairs, and once, when I sat with one space between us (too shy to sit beside her) she lifted her silk-stocking calves across my thighs and said with a cheeky grin, "May I?" But Deirdre was already my girlfriend, the ground beneath my feet, while Eva, who I'd hardly spoken to, was the moon and stars.

I wanted sex with Deirdre, but in that pre-pill purgatory condoms weren't handed out free by GPs or displayed in supermarkets, and I had yet to overcome the blushing embarrassment of asking the barber for something for the weekend. The female form too was a mystery (naughty pictures were airbrushed to look like Victorian paintings), and although when Deirdre wore tight trousers I studied the curves of her lower body I could never quite picture her naked. Sometimes when my parents were out she consented to come up to my bedroom, where after she had tidied up my scattered clothes and books (I can almost hear her voice asking which drawer some item belonged in) we lay on my bed together and kissed and cuddled. Sometimes she allowed me to put my hand (if I warmed it) *inside* her jumper, but if I tried to lift her skirt she laid a cold hand on mine and whispered, "No." So it was surprising when one day something changed.

But all that is long ago, and after a life of work in various countries, where Eva studied the local textiles and folk patterns and I took photographs for the books we wrote together, and decades of work on this smallholding which will now go back to nature when we sell our Jacobs sheep and angora goats, we have given up spinning and dyeing wool, and a few chickens will be our only companions. Our parents have died, our children left home long ago to raise children of their own, and although the good earth may soon swallow us we accept our end knowing we made the very most of our life together. So here I lie daydreaming under the night sky (cloud is hiding most of the stars now) until Eva turns off the light in her studio and calls me to join her for our nightcap.

When our parents die we step into the front rank facing death. I liked Eva's parents, her father who repaired stringed instruments and whose workshop smelled of hot fish glue and wax and shavings of aromatic hardwood, her mother who had sung in opera and now gave lessons to pale intense aspiring singers, in that cluttered converted Victorian schoolhouse on the edge of our industrial town, where the high peat moors rolled to the skyline and sometimes favoured the breeze with the scent of sphagnum moss.

Deirdre's parents' suburb was in the same town but felt like a different country. Neat nineteen-thirties Ideal Home Exhibition semis, around a green, kept moors and mills at a distance. When I went in through their front door I was greeted by a strong aroma of air freshener. The parents, who both worked for the local bus company, he as an inspector, she in the finance department, looked at me with suspicion as if divining my desire to seduce their daughter. They approved of my apprenticeship in a mill machinery firm, but looked worried when I brushed off their enquiries about my ultimate ambitions. I was never at ease with them. Eva's parents—I was going to say 'accepted' me, but that implies some kind of transition, whereas the first time I met George in his workshop he started on to me about the seasoning of oak as if continuing a previous conversation. As for her mother, Grace, her first words to me, after finishing the piece she was playing on the piano and standing to kiss me on both cheeks, were, "I see you like Satie, Peter."

My memory is unreliable now. Was it Grace who urged me to do the same course in textile design that Eva was taking? Or was it Eva herself? Never mind. All that matters is that the projects we've collaborated on have been as numerous as … what? As the stars I still see between the spreading clouds? And if I hadn't held back that day with Deirdre, I might be somewhere else in a very different life.

We were on my bed, engaged in the usual skirmishing, but somehow something had changed. Was Deirdre aware of my growing interest in Eva? The fact was that when I lifted her skirt, for once I met no resistance. She squeezed her eyes shut with a slight movement of her head, her fair hair contrasting with the dark blue of my pillow. I was in a state of excitement. It was the first time I had stroked the tender skin of a girl's inner thighs above her stocking tops, and through soft fabric the surprising hardness of her mound of Venus. I hooked my fingers into the elastic of her panties, the smooth skin of her belly against my knuckles, and gently drew them off her. I paused, expecting some protest, but she merely sighed.

And then again something changed. Let me try to remember this clearly. I think I was about to undo my trousers, but the thought of entering her must have been blocked by another. If I carried on without precautions and made her pregnant, I would have to marry her. Did I really want to be committed to this girl ('I liked her a lot' as the song says) who was a good enough companion, whose body attracted me, but whose conversation compared with Eva's was less than thrilling? On the other hand, excitement made me long to proceed, to touch the core of her womanhood (I already scented a change in her) and put a *dénouement* to our irritating fumblings.

I thank heaven that I held back. The details are hazy, but I know my restraint must have cost an effort worthy of Saint Anthony. What I remember clearly is standing by the bed fastening my trousers while Deirdre stared at me with an expression on her face I had never seen before, a congested, misty-eyed look. I kissed her and murmured something, probably that I respected her too much to take such a serious matter lightly, and then I was free, free to be with Eva for a lifetime of challenge and joy.

Sometimes in the heat of some desert I have now revisited on TV, with an irritating commentary by some self-satisfied bastard being paid for the privilege, I would stop and wonder, with the Atacama, the Sonora, or the fringe of the Sahara all round me, what life with Deirdre would have been like. We would certainly have stayed in that northern suburb to be near her parents and cousins, and instead of studying textile design and writing books with Eva I would have been drawn into working for the bus company (the mills having closed when the cotton industry moved east). I would be retired from the post of depot inspector inherited from my father-in-law. Oh, it's an honourable job—buses have to run, taking folks to work or to go and see their auntie—but my furthest horizons would be Bolton and Halifax, the limits of the company's bus routes (apart from the odd Blackpool run) instead of the remote parts of other continents. I might be secretary of the local bowls club, while Deirdre walked our two Labradors. I would be flayed by the memory of Eva's grey eyes piercing my soul as I walked away from her to marry Deirdre. Instead it was Deirdre I walked away from — the details are no longer clear — to marry Eva in a fairytale wedding, our lovemaking like a dream, our lives together blossoming.

Our garden featured recently on *Gardener's World*. There they were, all the plants we collected on our travels flanking that sunlit curving path we sweated to create, the hebes and euonymus glowing with pride, and there in close-up were the lilies, her great enthusiasm, and Eva herself (suddenly older than I'd realised, having seen her change so gradually from day to day), with that characteristic curl to those lovely lips and the energy she puts into the least remark. Yes, our garden, created with much digging and barrowing and agonising over choices until one day we could stand wiping our brows with our arms around one another, suddenly thinking, Done!

And the visitors came, in ones and twos, then coachloads. Some have just arrived, I think, because I hear voices and the sound of a trolley, which means someone is buying plants from our nursery, listening to Eva explain about semi-shade and alkaline soil, although that voice isn't Eva's — maybe it's that foreign girl who sometimes helps.

The night is over now. There's brightness but little warmth, and without my glasses I can't really see the sky. Strangely the recliner I'm on is moving, and one of our visitors in some uniform (an off-duty nurse, perhaps?) is looking down at me. I must call to Eva and ask what's happening, but ah, no need, because the visitor is saying, "Peter, your wife's here." And Eva's hand is on my arm, but I need my glasses to see her face.

"My glasses! My glasses!" I murmur, and someone puts them on me, and there smiling down at me is my wife Deirdre. "You've had the operation, Peter," she's saying. "Your heart is mended."

Creels

Jane, Christopher, you wouldn't believe how I've agonised over this. Which is ridiculous—I might never post it. It may not arrive. Or you may not be ready to read it, and find it after thirty years in a world of different people.

You may not remember what I look like, and I'm old now. A woman of seventy, less tall but still strong, with long unruly hair not entirely grey. I rarely look in a mirror, afraid it will crack. But the window in front of my work table reflects a vague outline.

That window looks onto a quayside where fishing boats are moored. There are creels piled everywhere. The rounded ends with crisscross ropework must seep into my brain, because they're often a motif in my work. I would very much like to give you one of my embroidered wall hangings. They're in demand, so it would be a real gift, not an unburdening.

On my right another window looks onto a small garden filled with colourful annuals. It's triangular, bounded by the quayside and a road that converges with it. Don't worry if that's hard to imagine. If only you could come here and see it! But life is full of if-onlys.

The road is piled with creels like the quayside. In the distance is a flagpole. The blue flag with its white diagonal cross is tugging at its rope, as if to escape. Some mornings the sun sprinkles the sea with a million lights, and pours through the window to warm me as I work. Then moves to warm me through the other window. But usually clouds intervene. And often the wind moans and the sun never appears.

What do I think about as I work? On the wall in front of me hangs a photograph, your frozen selves in a moment long gone. Sometimes a movement on the edge of my vision tells me a fishing boat is heading out. This reminds me of the toy fishing boats I once bought you, which on my last visit I found in your garden, broken. But I don't pursue that thought.

Sometimes I think of your Grandpa, and how my life once had another dimension, of trees laden with apples, days filled with the rhythm of work, evenings rich with possibilities. His photo hangs near yours, never changing. Jane and Christopher, try to remember him.

A friend from the village, another artist, has just dropped in for coffee. I wanted to share this writing with her, but lacked the courage. And I wish I'd told her about my last visit to your father.

Ben lives — you may not know — in a mountain village in northern Greece. The scent of hot pine trees, the taste of fresh olives, frame our last encounter. He hid his eyes with sunglasses. He and his Greek friends played endless games of backgammon. The Euros piled up his side of the table. He said his success was based on probabilities. 'Suppose you need a six to hit an opponent's blot. What are the odds of getting it?' He wrote all possible die combinations on the café menu. 'There — the odds are seventeen divided by thirty-six.' All this in his head of course — he only wrote it down for me.

I tried to discuss you with him, but not even his Greek friends could persuade him to take me seriously. You must understand that your father has suffered — through nobody's fault — and learned to defend himself behind a stubborn wall. Perhaps he feels he doesn't deserve you. But I deserve you, Jane and Christopher. I do.

I hope I'm a good person. And in case you get me wrong, I think Kay and Roger are good people. For reasons too deep to fathom, good people don't always understand one another. One night Kay and I sat up till two. This was early on, soon after Ben's breakdown, and before Roger.

Kay was in her white fluffy dressing-gown with the purple and orange spots. I was in my old nightie with a tartan blanket. The traffic slowly faded from a grumble to a whisper. I found it hard being in a city. We listened to Andrea Bocelli. She made cocoa, which we kept allowing to go cold, so she had to warm it again.

She kept sighing, "I don't know."

"What don't you know, Kay?"

She talked on as if to herself. Whenever I replied she looked at me as if I'd appeared by magic. She brushed her blonde hair off her face with a distracted gesture. Each time the CD ended she started it again. If I listen to those songs now I feel the chill of knowing there was nothing to be said.

Night has fallen in this village far from your home. I drew the curtain on the south window but left the east window bare. I have eaten a simple meal and am ready for the task I couldn't face before. To record my last visit.

I arrived after a long drive and was greeted by … No, no, I have to tell it as if I'm someone else.

The woman arrives and is greeted by Kay and Roger. Roger introduces himself in a friendly way, asks about her journey, and makes sympathetic remarks about long drives. Then stands back, stroking his beard, weighing up this person he's heard about. Kay is wary, fingering her beads. Baltic amber, a present the woman gave her before she married Ben.

The afternoon passes calmly. The adults join you children to watch cartoons. Then the woman is given the privilege of reading you a bedtime story. She thinks something you hardly understand is the best sleep-inducer, so reads *Four Quartets*. And, bless you, you listen, perhaps absorbing the rhythms. Kay meanwhile has dinner ready, but is loath to interrupt the sleep process. After another half hour, though, she hurries up to check.

The two of you have been fast asleep for some time, little angels' heads on white pillows. Kay's heart catches at the sight of you, so vulnerable and precious. The woman, leaning over you like an alien presence, is halfway through reading *Little Gidding*. There's something disturbing about the way she looks at you, as if you not dinner were on the menu.

The meal goes well enough. Kay mentions the reading matter, and the woman is embarrassed, but Roger laughs and defuses the tension. There's polite conversation about gardening, the state of Highland roads, the uncertainties of mobile signals. The woman has brought a present of whisky, from a distillery on her route south, and the three of them settle down to sample it. It's 'cask strength', more potent than they realise. The conversation moves on to higher education. Yours. Should Kay and Roger one day move back north of the Border? Of course, that's way in the future, and the future is an icy hand stroking the woman's heart.

Roger is speaking. "Too many youngsters apply to universities when they'd be better off going straight into work."

"Straight into unemployment," says Kay.

"Well at least they won't have unreal expectations."

Kay shrugs. The woman frowns, anxious in case an argument is brewing. Roger asks what she thinks.

"I don't have much experience of the issues."

"But your son went to university. And did well. A First in mathematics. Was he motivated? Did you and your husband have to push him?"

"*Push* him?"

Kay says, "He doesn't mean pushed, he means encouraged. Don't you, Rog?"

Roger waits for the woman's answer. She takes too big a swig of the spirits and starts coughing. This brings tears to her eyes. It's just a physiological reaction.

She says, "You think that's why he had a breakdown. That I couldn't rest until he could call himself 'Doctor'. That it's all my fault."

Your mother and stepfather shake their heads and murmur, "No, no," but there's a kind of volcanic eruption in the woman's chest.

She goes on, "If someone goes off the rails people look at the parents. Oh my God, what did they do wrong? Not enough love, not enough discipline, unhappy-marriage debris piled on the little ones' heads. Well I hope you two are never in that position. But I can tell you, neither John nor I pushed Ben to do a PhD when he already had children."

Kay has turned very pale and is shredding a red paper napkin. Crimson blobs litter the carpet.

"You think *I* pushed him."

She mutters this. The woman doesn't quite catch what she's saying and doesn't reply. By the time it registers, Kay has left the room. When she doesn't come back right away Roger goes to find her.

Oh they aren't out long. When they come back it's with cups of tea and polite smiles. They aren't in the least unfriendly. The chill in the room is just the onset of autumn. Next morning the woman offers to babysit while Kay and Roger go to work, but they tell her the children are expected at the day nursery, and anyway, with a long drive ahead of her, best get it done before dark.

Midnight. The dark presses against the window. Sometimes I fear it will burst through. But I keep the curtains open to see the lights on the fishing boats.

A few weeks ago I was on Facebook. I only use it to post pictures of my work. But somehow, through some mutual 'friend' I suppose, I came across Kay's mother. Suddenly, Jane and Christopher, I was looking at you.

One photo was at the beach. How you've grown! You were smiling, sunburnt, squinting into the sun. Another was a riding lesson, both of you very serious and important. Kay's mother held Christopher's pony's bridle, her father held Jane's. The caption read *Having a lovely time with our lovely grandchildren.*

I didn't post a comment. I went for a long walk. On the headland above the village is a high sheer cliff. I stood there a long time and listened to the sea, and the wind in the dry grasses. Then remembered the stone a friend says has been dowsed and draws magic from deep in the earth. I always thought this was nonsense, but I bent and touched it to send you my blessing.

I find this is my seventh letter. It's hard to remember the other six. I think I got stuck on one topic each time, something I thought would interest you. There was the Seagull Letter, the Seal Pup Letter, the Seaweed Letter … I don't know whether you read them, or had them read to you, or what you thought of your birthday and Christmas presents. Maybe the letters were unsuitable. Or unwelcome, like tar on the beach. And the presents tainted, attempts to arouse your gratitude or make you notice me.

Perhaps I should have overcome my fear and driven to see you when I still could. Now my hands are claws, useless for steering, but still able to wield a needle and scissors—just. I'm very slow! The good news is, that gives my work scarcity value. If you ever see my wall hangings you'll find them quite original. The grey of the sea goes into them, the duck-egg blue of the sky, and the brown of the creel netting, but I often add blobs of red, which sing out. One day I might portray a creel with a lobster in it, wondering how something easy to get into is impossible to escape.

Meanwhile, it's almost time to draw the curtains. I look at these hands and think I'm clawing my way into the future. Gales are forecast, but moving lights in the dark show one crew setting out regardless. Join me, Jane and Christopher, in wishing them safe passage. And give Kay and Roger my very best wishes. With all my love, your Grandma Ella.

Trouble

This feller's got trouble written all over him.

There he is at the counter with his back to me, ordering coffee in a rough voice. His body language is wrong, he's standing unnaturally still, and when he moves he lifts his arms jerkily like a puppet. And his clothes, they're wrong too. A tight wolf-skin-coloured anorak with two inches of jacket showing below it. Has he thrown on the first things he found? No, he's done it deliberately to make me stare, so he can stare back: 'Lookin' at me?'

You can bet your life he's going to sit near me. Not in the window by the two old women. Not in the corner by the young couple with the baby. See? Here he comes. Hair short all over. His face bad news just like the back of his head.

It doesn't matter that I'm minding my own business. Enjoying a cup of tea on the way home from a day's cycling. Reading headlines in the local rag—GIRL FIGHTS OFF PERVERT, MAN BEATEN IN SAVAGE ATTACK—the usual stuff. I knew it'd be with me that he'd have the problem.

He sits at the next table, eyes me up and down. That's how they start, his type—set you on edge, get you on the wrong foot. He's looking for something about me to comment on. My cycling shorts perhaps. Thinks I'm too old to wear them at fifty-three. So how old's he? Thirty I'd guess. Then why does he make me think of a kid of ten?

When I was ten Dad took me to his home town in Scotland.

Every day kids cornered me in the street outside my Grandad's. They sneered at my accent and spat incomprehensible insults. I knew they were insults from the tone. One lad started jostling me. Dad called from the window, "Sock him." I didn't. I never did, the whole week.

I was never afraid of a roughhouse. At home I scuffled with friends, wrestled, and shouted, "Pile on!" But in a real fight I was terrified of losing my temper. If someone cheated me or hit me with malice the blood would surge behind my eyeballs, I'd go OTT, roar like a demon, lunge at the enemy's eyes and balls. Afterwards I'd sit alone in the shed, drained and miserable, shaken by the thought of the damage I'd tried to do.

Dad taught me to box. Well, that's what he thought. What he did was dance round me and land hard slaps on my face barehanded.

"Come on, keep up your guard."

Wham, another slap. "Ow," I said.

"Move, ye've to keep moving."

Wham. "Ow."

"Duck, ye've to duck your head."

"I don't understand what you have to do."

When I grew up I did some judo. Learned how you have to concentrate your energy. Lost some of my fear of unknown men and their physical presence. Only got as far as orange belt, but winning that was a big step for me. On the way home from the grading meeting I called on Dad.

"Ye can hold your own now," he said.

"I don't know about that."

"Aye. A quick chop says who's boss."

I said, "That's karate. This is judo. It's just sport. It means 'the gentle art'."

He gave me an empty look and turned his attention back to the telly.

The feller's still looking me over. No shame, no uncertainty. I'll ignore him, read through the paper a second time. No, too depressing. Look at the plastic flowers, the menu.

No good. He leans towards me. I freeze.

He says, "I've just lost me dad."

There's a long pause. Then I say, "I'm very sorry."

"Can't gerrover it. I've not slept since yesterday."

"What happened?"

"He woke up with a headache. Three hours later they took him in. Ten hours later he was dead. A massive brain haemorrhage."

Now we look at each other straight. His face is like a medieval carving I saw in Germany. One of the crucified thieves. Scored with deep vertical lines, nose and forehead bony. His eyes, rimmed with red between swollen pillows of flesh, droop at the outside edges as if weighted.

"Was it unexpected?" I ask.

"Totally."

"Must have been a terrible shock."

His eyes lose focus. "Can't go for a pint with him no more. Can't go and say, 'Hey, Dad, lend us a fiver.'" He twists his hand down and holds it out backwards to illustrate. "I mean, your dad's your best friend, isn't he?"

The waitress brings more coffee which saves me thinking of a reply. He stirs it with a distant look, like someone just hauled from a shipwreck, but his eyes have filled.

"I'm at war with Jesus," he says. "For taking him."

There's no answer to that. Jesus and I lost touch some time ago. Dad still goes to church when someone'll take him. Maybe he prays for me, who knows?

I ask, "Is your mother living?"

"Yeah. She can't cope, doesn't know where she is. She's on tranquillisers." And as if he's just remembered, with mild surprise, "So am I." He looks straight at me again. "He wouldn't have suffered, would he?"

"No."

"Wouldn't have felt no pain."

"Not a thing."

He seems satisfied.

I ask, "How old was he?"

"Fifty-three."

Time to go. I pay the waitress and stand up with my saddlebag. My thighs are stiff. He looks up at me. I wish I could say, 'Sorry for your trouble,' but I'm not Irish.

"Bye then. I'm very sorry."

"Is your Dad alive?" he asks.

"Yes. But he's been that close to dying." I hold up finger and thumb an inch apart. "One time I really thought he'd gone."

"And I bet you cried."

I mutter something about Dad starting to recover before what was happening had sunk in. The feller nods and takes a swig of coffee.

"Yes," he says. "Yes, you'll have cried all right."

Whiskey and Halva

"Failure is instructive," Raj says.

"Because it makes me determined to succeed?"

Raj shakes his head. The fierce sun makes blue highlights in his hair. "Because you confront your ego, Dermot. That monkey on your shoulder."

"There's no monkey on my shoulder."

"Correction — an ape. Even more hard to shift."

Across the square a boy of about fifteen is shouting urgently, "*Soba, Aw Wadi, Aw Wadi.*" He bends forward, his pointing arm tense. But the bus he points to isn't one they need.

"So where *is* Mr Madi?" Dermot asks.

A forlorn question. It's clear they won't get to see the *Souk al Gamal*, the camel market, or the whirling dervishes. The slow time will go unfilled. Raj holds up his right hand with the fingers curved back, the gesture of an Indian dancer.

"I imagine he fails to achieve petrol. Thus sharing my own petrol failure, leaving us with failure to achieve our aim."

After another half hour it's back to the government rest house. Raj's heel-less shoes flap annoyingly.

On guard at Tahir's office, two policemen in dusty black uniforms. Inside, long corridors. Sand has blown in through open windows.

"Any boxes, Mr Tahir?"

"*Ma fi*, Mr Smeeth."

The desk fan blows dusty papers all over. The ad hoc paperweights don't help. One is a Tahini jar filled with sand. When Tahir stoops to retrieve his documents there's a round patch of sweat on the back of his shirt. Dermot thinks of the circles cut in the uniforms of prisoners-of-war.

"When's the next freight train?"

"*Ma fiish ghatr.*"

At the rest house Raj is back for lunch. Every morning he checks the freight section at the airport.

"You know there are no trains, Dermot. Heavy rain washed away the line from the port."

"I need to check. Do something."

Raj nods. He understands.

"So nothing at the airport, Raj? Big-end bearing shells?"

"No."

"Filter elements, carbon brushes, a decoke set?"

"Nothing. I am told every aircraft bombs the rebels. Or drops food to those unfortunates who flee the fighting."

Claire says, "You're being melodramatic, Dermot."

"Am I though?"

"You think you're some tragic hero. A character in a film."

Dermot makes a slow circuit of the room. Picks up a *cloisonné* vase that belonged to his grandmother and wonders what she'd think of this scene. He straightens a pile of books. The top one is *Ten Steps to Self-Improvement*. He picks a rubber band off the carpet. By the time he returns to his starting point nothing has changed.

Claire is in her dressing-gown, green winceyette. Scarlet varnish is wearing off her toenails. It makes them look diseased. She keeps looking at him, then away, studying the sky through the grimy window. Perhaps the right thing to say is written among the clouds. He thinks of kissing her, risking an outcry. He doesn't.

The rest house, Tahir's office, American Express — no other life. Every day he walks the six blocks to look for a letter, trembling. He imagines slitting the envelope and seeing the edge of something. Doom? When he tries with awkward fingers to pull it out it will catch and buckle. He'll unfold it, see the plain back first, then turn it over, breathless …

Sometime he walks in warm rain. Or after rain, everything steaming. Or when harsh sunlight makes palm-leaf shadows on roughcast walls. He passes huge pots with pointed bases on metal stands. Crowds of men around flaking kiosks buying Pepsi and Marlboros. Their dusty black faces contrast with the white of headcloths and *djellabias*.

So far, no letter.

"I shall go to San Giacomo College," says Raj. "It may be suitable for my son."

Evidently a Catholic school is next best to a Hindu one. Many saints, many gods, Dermot supposes.

"I wish you well with that, Raj."

"And someone should wish us well with generators. We cannot repair them when correct parts are lacking."

"And you can't rent a flat till your furniture arrives."

"Every day I pray to God."

"*One* God? I thought you had several."

Raj widens his eyes. The whites are very slightly bloodshot. "What else are you thinking, Dermot?"

"That you believe the world is supported by four elephants standing on the shell of a huge turtle."

"If this is what *you* believe, Dermot, no wonder you are confused." Raj says this without irony.

Often silence falls between them. Silent companionship. The ceiling fan throbs, as always except when there's a power-cut. Looking up Dermot sees himself reflected at its centre like someone down in a well.

"Okay, Raj. Do you believe in rebirth?"

"Yes, because you know that *Bireddin*? He was valet to a bishop. And now is reborn as our *dhobi wallah*."

"Raj?"

"Yes?"

"Why do you mispronounce my name? It's not 'Dare-mot'."

Raj grins. "But it has to rhyme with 'Dare not'."

Claire says, "I'm ashamed, all right? I fell. You weren't here. I didn't hear from you. I didn't know when you'd be back from South America. *If* you'd be back."

"It was hard to phone from where I was. I arrived from the airport to a locked house, keys buried in my luggage. So I went to Ryan's Bar and tried two hours later. You looked shocked, as if I was a stranger. Which I suppose I was."

"I don't know."

"You didn't hug or kiss me. The house felt empty."

Claire sighs and squeezes her eyes shut.

Dermot says, "I soon picked up on the signs. Your hushed tone when your boss rang, the bed not slept in, your ... awkwardness."

"All right! He's divorced. I was staying with him."

"So what happens now?"

"Nothing, Dermot. That interlude is over."

Details kill you, Dermot thinks. The word 'interlude' maddens him. They both start shouting at once. Hurt by a partner's absence! Stressed by a demanding job! Anger makes

92

Claire's bosom heave. Dermot thinks of her boss fondling her breasts. Her normally pale face is crimson, ill-matched with the rust red of her hair.

Raj invites Dermot to the India Club.

"But you can't get petrol."

"We will take a *boxi*."

"They don't stop for Europeans. I've tried."

"I will be with you."

The smell of hot oil, the rattle of the truck's bodywork, the unintelligible conversation all around, make Dermot feel free to speak.

"While I was on a job in South America, Claire had an affair."

"Who is that Claire?"

"I told you."

"She who sends no letter. Even though the same spirit is in both of you."

Dermot isn't in the mood for mystical stuff. Except maybe the giant tortoise.

A tall man with a brown polished face and neat moustache leans across the narrow gangway and exchanges words with Raj in Urdu. Not that different from Hindi, it seems. The man turns to Dermot.

"Excuse my overhearing your mention of adultery. I am Dr Aftab Salik, University Department of Econometrics. You should know that, in my country, adulterous woman receives forty vips."

"Whips?"

"Yes, vips."

"And if it was because she was lonely and distressed?"

Dr Salik thinks for a moment. "Thirty-nine vips."

The bustle of arrival cuts this conversation. Alighting in an unfamiliar street near the central market, Dermot steps on a cast-iron manhole cover. In the sun-gilded dust raised by the *boxi*, amid the clamour of voices and the flitting of black limbs in white robes, he reads letters raised in the metal, polished by passing feet.

"Raj! Raj! Look! My uncle went to work in that foundry. It's in a town in the North of England."

Raj laughs. "A relic of British rule. These people took too long to shake the buggers off. We Indians beat them to it."

"And so," says Dermot, "did we."

Met my love by the gasworks wall/Dreamed a dream by the old canal … Vents in the dirty brick-arched windows issued plumes, reflected in the canal. Familiar from childhood visits with his father. The interior smelt of smoke and burnt grease and hot sand. Men in sweat-stained vests made crimson spouts from the bowls of long ladles. Streams of molten iron so bright they belonged in a different world.

One moment the liquid could become anything. The next it cooled to a shape only shattering could alter. There was beauty in the virgin shine of those newborn castings. With lettering and lozenge shapes proud of the surface and keyholes to fit the long rods of men in peaked caps. The umbilical sprue of those manhole covers was yet to be ground off, patina had yet to dull them.

And here, in this baking city with its dark smell of decay and earth, its ochre streets whose blank buildings turn inwards in sanctified privacy, is one of them.

Afternoons in the rest house. No pattern. He stares at the walls, counts lizards. Reads books he wouldn't read at home. Calls Abdallah—'*Ya Abdallah!*'—to make a cup of tea, and disturbing him at prayer feels guilty.

The *Ya Abdallah* habit is from Raj, who is used to servants.

When his furniture and effects arrive from Libya he can leave the rest house and his wife and children can join him.

"Glad *I* didn't lumber myself with a family."

"Not married, Dermot?"

"No, Raj. And I've just left my partner."

"But you expect a letter."

"There won't be one."

"Yet you go often to American Express to look."

"There's damn all useful she can say."

"Usefulness is required by practical men. And you do not telephone." He nods. "Always there is suffering."

"Do you miss your wife and kids?"

Raj says nothing.

Every evening meal in the rest house is the same: meat chunks, okra, potato, spicy sauce, followed by green bananas. Afterwards they stroll around the diplomatic quarter. Quiet streets, lush squares of garden behind high steel fences. The slap of Raj's shoes. Then back to the rest house for whiskey and halva and biscuits, and Raj sighing, 'Ah, not very bad.' A supper Dermot grows to dislike. But if he misses it or the walk he feels bereft.

If there's a power cut the overhead fan stops and the heat builds.

"If parts would come we could fix a few generators."

"The days are endless, Raj."

Sunday. A work day, because Friday is Sunday here. After his usual breakfast of *fûl* beans, scrambled egg, and milky coffee, Dermot goes out, walking fast beside the river. It rained again in the night, washing down the dust, and the air is clear and fresh.

He reaches the head post office and stands for a moment before going in. Normally he's afraid to hesitate, in case he loses his sense of purpose, but this is just the brief silence between movements of a concerto. On the outside wall of the building are two neon tubes in a V, unprotected from weather. Dermot smiles at a boy in an openwork skull-cap on a donkey. The boy salutes and rides by, his load bumping on the beast's sweaty flanks.

In the lobby with its row of dimly-lit phone cubicles, Dermot joins the crowd at the counter. He books a call to Claire and waits. An hour goes by. He's in a trance, one more body in a crowd.

The counter clerk says, "Mr Smeeth, cubicle two."

Dermot turns and hurries out.

Suddenly there are three under the evening fan. Dermot imagined Russian women with sweet round faces like *Matryoshka* dolls, but Valentina's is a blade. Her eyes, dark and wide, move from him to Raj and back, as if either might solve some enigma.

"Where were you working before?" Dermot asks.

"Finland."

"In what capacity?" Raj asks.

"Educational."

"And before Finland?"

"Morocco. Bulgaria."

Her tone is flat, as if Bulgaria is just like Morocco, and Morocco just like Finland.

Raj is fascinated by her. Under the blaze of her questioning look he lowers his eyes, but when she moves he studies her intently.

"She favours you," he says later over whiskey and halva, when Valentina has gone to bed.

"She just thinks I follow her broken English better."

"Yet Russian," says Raj with the nearest to bitterness Dermot has heard from him, "is closer to Hindi than to English."

Ramadan. Raj is in India touching base with his head office. Dermot and Valentina cross to an island in the river. The cheapest ferry trip in the world, according to the boatman. The earth is pungent after rain. They walk along quiet humble streets between earth walls, then the banked edges of irrigated fields, and look back at the city skyline. Pale rectangles, plum-coloured minarets. At dusk smiling men breaking their fast beckon them to share fresh lemonade.

Back at the rest house Dermot and Valentina sit at the table under the fan, sharing a bottle of sparkling water. It's warm and tastes unpleasant. Valentina's eyes search his face. He knows what's expected. To ask about her hopes and fears, her lovers, tell her she looks nice, then take her to bed. Only fair. It would balance Claire's betrayal.

But a cloak of lead has descended. Dermot sees every stage of what's supposed to happen, in tiny increments like Achilles and the tortoise. The uncovering of bodies, the sweat-sticky coupling, the post-coital anxiety over whether they respect each other and how it might all develop. All he wants is the stage where bodies lie close drained of passion and conversation, but there are too many steps to reach it. He can almost understand why Claire slept with Daniel.

He pats the hand Valentina has stretched towards him and says, "I have to leave you now. Goodnight." Her eyes are huge, her face a hatchet.

From his room he looks down at the street, drowned in shadows. The shops are blank, with steel shutters like prison doors. It's late, very late, before he sleeps.

The earth steams with the ancient smells of *Ur* and *Mohenjo-Daro*. In a sea of semi-darkness the stalls are islands of electric light. Between them squat people with few things to sell — belts, extension leads, handfuls of cigarettes. Snatches of music swoop like Arabic writing. A fingerless beggar really does say *baksheesh*, and he gives her a banknote, limp with the sweat of many hands.

By the meat market the odour is sickening. The primitive squalor fits his thoughts. Men in white robes and bulky head cloths slap one another's hands in greeting. He's fascinated by a heap of dung—which may even be human—and the jewelled backs of its attendant flies. He gazes long. A gentle tap on his shoulder. It's Raj.

Dermot pumps his hand like mad.

"Back from India! Good to see you."

"I think parts do not come?"

"Correct. And your furniture?"

Again the dancer's gesture. "It is promised."

They stroll along together. Raj is visiting a shop in the Goldsmiths' quarter.

"And how is that Claire?" he asks.

"No letter. And no, I haven't phoned."

"Interesting."

'What's interesting, Raj?"

"That I find you looking into a pile of *ordure*. Instead of into yourself."

"And if I did," Dermot says sarcastically, "what would I see?"

But they've arrived. Outside the shop an argument is in progress between Raj's friend and an angry customer. In Hindi, with occasional bursts of English. Raj explains that English is for emphasis. The dispute shows no sign of ending. It seems both parties are enjoying it. Raj and Dermot drift away.

The air is unusually humid after the rain. The risen moon slides among the fans of palm trees.

"Fear," says Raj suddenly.

"What?"

"You would see fear inside you."

"Fear of what will happen if I phone Claire?"

Raj shrugs.

"What do *you* think will happen?" Dermot demands.

Raj walks on deep in thought, shoes flapping as usual. Dermot is on edge for his answer. The oracle!

"Tell me, Dermot," says Raj at last, "when you came here, were you knowing what would happen?"

Dermot thinks angrily, Where is that Eastern wisdom?

The police wielding *lathis* force back the crowd.

"Come," says Raj. Firmly, because he sees Dermot is reluctant. Embarrassed. Letting in a brown man and a white man before the black locals is a vestige of colonial days.

The film has subtitles in Arabic and English. The hero is a police detective but looks like a playboy. He never gets angry. With men he's blunt, matter-of fact — if they don't co-operate there'll be consequences. Sometimes he drawls in English, 'You are very big wicked man.' With women he's kind and charming, but firm. If they get angry he shrugs — they have to accept him as he is.

And he dances! And sings! In front of a crowd of dancers in shiny costumes, grinning at the camera, hands expressive. Dermot sneaks a look at Raj. His companion's dark eyes are moist. Dermot looks away quickly. The night is warm, his shirt clings to his back with sweat, but it's good to be in the open and the bench under his thighs feels very solid.

They stroll back to the rest house.

"Surely," says Dermot, "a song and dance routine is odd in a detective story."

Raj holds one hand upright at right angles to his lips — thinking mode. "Tell me, Dermot," he murmurs, "why you became an engineer."

"I like solving problems. Problem solving is the essence of being human."

Raj nods gravely. "Agreed. But what of *insoluble* problems?"

"What about them?"

"Are they not windows into the divine?"

He laughs at Dermot's puzzled look. They walk on.

"Now tell me, Dermot, when solving problem, do you sometimes stand back, away from problem, to rest?"

"Sometimes."

"That is your dance."

And Raj laughs again, for quite a long time.

Dermot is still thinking about the film. It ends with the detective picking up a phone. He hesitates. The call is to a politician. Is it wise? Ominous music. But the hero dials, and someone answers.

Snaps

"Well I sure hope we find them," the American woman says.

"Right," says her husband with a stern look at Carlos. Who in turn peers through the taxi window at the scrubby, half-tropical landscape, trying to look like someone who Knows Indians.

The Englishman is quiet. He can't get over how much this feels like a Sunday morning. Not just the old kind, the newspaper-and-croissants kind, with a walk by the river with his wife, but the oldest kind. When there was a sense of aimlessness and space, of not knowing what would happen next. Of strolling home from church with Bonesie and Rob, going miles out of their way, just in case they crossed the path (by pure accident) of Ann Bell and Jennifer Coates.

They cross a bridge, heavy tree-trunks laid crosswise with planks. Under it a small ravine. Carlos scans the overcast sky, the tops of the grey-green palm trees, for clues. The driver turns left into a large clearing, and pulls up in front of a large shed-like building. It has plank walls and a tin roof. The Americans think of the hut at Fifth and Maple where they used to take LaVerne for ballet. In that strange, disturbing area just off the main centre, not quite yet decayed enough to tear down.

The husband balances his camcorder on his knee and wipes the sweat off his palms onto his shirt. His wife looks away, silently disapproving. "There's no-one here," she tells Carlos. The building seems deserted. Carlos too is sweating. He's brought them all the way from Quito to see these damned Colorado Indians. Booked them into the hotel he'd come to every weekend if he could afford it, only to find they aren't impressed. Sauna, swimming-pool, disco—what more can they want? They complain that the disco keeps them awake. He wonders what hotels in America are like, or Britain. At this rate he'll never know.

He and the taxi driver approach the door. The driver knocks.

Carlos asks, 'Who lives here?'

"The *brujo*."

Carlos wonders aloud how to render this in English. Witch-doctor? Herbalist?

The driver grins. "You should know, being a tour guide."

"I'm not a guide, I'm an engineer."

"Just moonlighting, eh? Well this could be a bad day. They may have just had a party. They drink and dance for days, then spend more days sleeping it off."

"Damn. I have to find them."

A young man in jeans and T-shirt answers the door. The son of the *brujo*. He has pale skin and fair hair, a contrast with the driver and Carlos. He directs them to another house. As they walk back to the taxi the driver says, "He could pass for a *gringo*."

"If he spoke English."

They drive on. Carlos, to entertain his party, points out banana and palm trees by the roadside. The American points his camcorder. His wife asks what kind of palm they are. They aren't neat and bushy like the ones in California. The lead shoots pop up from the rest with a leggy look, crowned with four leaves like small windmill sails. Also they aren't labelled like the ones in the arboretum.

"What species are those?" she asks.

Carlos says, "We call them *palmas*."

She thinks, He doesn't even know the word 'palm' in English.

The road gets worse. They cross a small river in which people are bathing and washing clothes. Everyone peers from the taxi, but the scene looks very ordinary.

The Englishman thinks of small rivers in France, he and his wife wading among the boulders, cooling off in the deep pools, laughing and pushing each other off balance. The light coming through leaves. Now she can hardly move. Her joints are going. They thought this trip would distract her from the pain, that the heat would help, but it isn't that warm on the Equator. She's hobbling around their apartment back in Quito.

"You go," she said. "I'll stay."

"Not on my own."

"You won't be on your own. You'll be with Carlos." And when he hesitated, "For God's sake, go."

Last night, at the disco, he and Carlos watched some young women dancing. The Americans stayed for one drink, then went to bed.

"Ask one to dance," said Carlos.

Seeing himself through their eyes, the Englishman feels old. He remembers his wife at parties deep in the past, weaving herself into the music, a blur of ankles. These girls are hardly moving.

Carlos adds, "Please, they like Englishmen. They think we Ecuadorian men are a lost cause."

"Never. Ask one yourself."

Carlos, his olive skin a little flushed, leans towards him. "I used to have an English girlfriend. I would like to go to UK, do a Master's."

The Englishman doesn't know what to say. He feels he

should offer him a room in their house. The children have left, the house is half empty. A haunted house, full of memories.

The taxi suddenly swings into another clearing, past a sign in Spanish: 'Tourists Welcome'. Carlos watches his party anxiously. To his relief the Americans' eyes light up: this is what they came for. A house in the local style, thatched with palm leaves. They get out quickly with relief, with a multiple thud of doors. The husband sweeps with his camcorder the enclosing ring of foliage, a dark, deep-green mass receding into mist, a mist that hints at reserves of tropical heat. He takes in bright scarlet flowers, cocoa trees, banana trees, shrubs of all kinds. And can't believe his delight when the shot comes back to the house, and there is the Indian.

The party all move towards him — apart from the driver of course, who's seen it all. The Americans catch one another's eyes and smile. The wife thinks how it would tickle LaVerne to see this guy, so unashamedly posing. Because she always enjoyed a spectacle, something to see, an old silver mine, a pretend gunfight, a valley full of weird-shaped mesas. Always so keen, bubbly, and bouncy.

She'd say, "This gets an A. I never *imagined* it like this. Now what?"

Because there was always something else to move on to.

What's great about the Indian, thinks the husband, is that he looks just like the photographs. The ones in the display at the Equator Monument. His hair really is this amazing shade of crimson. Shaved up the back and way above the ears, it's like a bowl inverted on his head. Smeared with some sticky plant goo, so thick it appears polished.

He seems quite at ease. Clearly poses like this every Sunday morning, in nothing but a yellow shirt (open to expose his chest and ample belly) and a smart striped wraparound in black and white. Standing with his feet at ten to two, with a faint grin, looking at the donkey-coloured earth in front of him. His legs are hairless and surprisingly white.

The visitors stand round in a half circle. Carlos is pleased. He'll interpret now, the fulcrum of the occasion. These people are in his power and will thank him. He met them on different days, in the tourist café on Avenida Amazonas. Made friends, offered this tour, agreed on a sum of money. Things here are so cheap for them that after meals, the hotel, buses, this taxi, he'll have a fair sum left over. Also, they agreed to pay for him. When he told them the cost of the weekend, and added, "Also the same for me," they nodded. But he isn't just a guide, he's a friend. One day, in the States or Britain, he'll meet another of those fugitive long-legged girls with rosy skin.

"You can question him through me," he says.

The Englishman looks at the slatted door of the house, at the gap above. Inside, darkness. Perhaps the Indian's wife is in there, lying sick. After all, they have no real doctors. The house has been spoiled by the debris of progress. An ugly electrical fuse-box on one bamboo column. On the door a Lufthansa sticker, an Ecuador Tourist Board sign, and inexplicably, a coloured picture of a railway train. But also, more hopefully, a record of the past. A sepia photograph of soldiers and Colorados.

He asks, "What's the photograph?"

The Indian explains, through Carlos, that the soldiers came to hunt some bad men who killed two Colorados. The American woman isn't satisfied with this.

"Killed them? Why?"

She doesn't like mysteries. Like the photos she found in LaVerne's hold-all, strange bearded men, hawk-like women, LaVerne bunched in with them. Who were they? she demanded. Well, in the end they found out. After a fashion.

Her husband says, "Tell him we know about many kinds of Indians. Many tribes. We've seen them in many places."

The Indian, hearing this translated, nods politely.

The American woman says, "I guess he's seen many kinds of Americans, dear. Carlos, how many of them are there?"

Carlos answers without reference to the Indian. He knows from the taxi-driver. "One thousand. The young do not desire to be Colorados. They think they have a bad reputation."

"And do they?"

"Not really."

The Indian continues to pose, unruffled even though questions have stopped getting through to him. Carlos wishes he himself could be so at ease, half-naked with just a wraparound. Sometimes, when he came from his bath with a towel round him, his girlfriend would pull it off, laughing. He'd always turn away instinctively, and she'd ask, "Why can't I see you?" In the end she went back to Bradford.

The American woman notices the Indian's bead necklace. Maybe that was it with LaVerne, some kind of voodoo, the necklace those people gave her. She pokes at the fellow's beads. "Where from?"

Carlos interprets. "The sea."

The Englishman wonders how she can be so lacking in tact. The Indian is on the defensive now, just maintaining his dignity under the prodding. Something has gone slightly out of key, as it always does. Things start well and then decline. This man has appeared from a different past, unimaginable, running as a child through dark green leaves, playing with palm branches, speaking a fluid language. Only to emerge into this clearing to be judged by foreigners.

Carlos worries that the Englishman looks bored. He indicates the banana trees around the clearing.

"Bananas."

"Yes. Thank you."

The Americans too are losing interest. They've come all the way from Quito to see a man with crimson hair, but there's a limit to how long such a thing can entertain. Carlos looks under the space in front of the house, where the roof sails over to form a canopy. Ah, there's a marimba, bamboo tubes hanging from split bamboo slats. He plays random notes, nods to the American to run his camcorder, plays to the lens. He motions the Englishman to use his camera too. The Englishman doesn't move. Meanwhile the American woman is studying the bushes.

"What are they called?"

The taxi-driver, dozing at his wheel, stirs and calls out to Carlos, "Those are the seeds they dye their hair with."

Carlos, inspired, tears off a branch and offers it to the woman. The Englishman looks at the Indian. Is he offended at having his garden pillaged? No, this is a different culture. Or maybe he accepts that from now on things can only get worse, slide into chaos. His life emptying out.

The American woman tears open the hairy seed, exposing something bright red and sticky. She thinks, Good, I've got to the bottom of this. She hands it round. She asks, "Do the women paint their hair?" The answer comes: "No. And not the young people either."

The Englishman suddenly bursts out laughing. His companions all stare at him. He's hardly shown any feelings the whole weekend. He says, "I'm sorry, it just seems funny. That at home young people do strange things to their hair to set them apart from adults. And here it's the reverse." He asks the Americans, "Don't you think so?"

They move away from him. There's something a little unbalanced about his laughter. Only the Indian is smiling, but he's been smiling all the time, gazing modestly at the ground, looking like some kind of idol. The American examines the house: a frame of heavy bamboo, faced with smaller, split bamboos. Good, he thinks, solid, you need a solid house. Young people don't always recognise that, but sooner or later they always learn. Get your priorities right and life won't kick you in the butt.

The slatted door to the dark opens, the Indian's wife comes out. Small, with a thin face and high cheekbones. She too wears a striped wraparound, longer than her husband's. Above, just a few strings of beads and a see-through shawl. Her long hair is loose and black, unpainted. The camcorder whirrs.

Now there are two of them, posing together.

The Englishman feels a stab of pain. So she isn't sick indoors, despite the only doctor being a hung-over *brujo*. She isn't young, but her skin hasn't lost its polish. The atmosphere in the clearing has changed. No longer a lone Indian but a couple, standing together, half-naked, smiling at nothing. Soon they'll have the clearing to themselves, the visitors gone like rain. The Englishman takes a quick photograph and turns away.

Carlos is relieved. The Americans too seem to have had enough. They can all go back to the hotel. He can have a swim before lunch, and see if that Russian woman is still there. He can see what she looks like in daylight, in a bikini. Everyone's looking round the clearing, pretending not to look at the taxi. There are no birds or animals.

He says, "You must pay them." This is what the driver told him. "One thousand sucres each." He wipes his brow. The day is heating up. The Englishman and American eye him coldly. He can't think why. A thousand sucres is a straw to them.

The American says, "I thought this was included?"

The Englishman nods. "So did I. I thought everything was included. How much did the bus and taxi cost you, anyway?"

"And the hotel," says the American. "I saw the tariff. How much are you making on this?"

The two foreigners look at each other appreciatively. Both travellers. They know the score. But the American woman mutters, "Please, no scenes, I can't stand scenes."

The Englishman says, "Let's have it out with him later."

"Right."

They're feeling grudgingly in their pockets when the door opens again and a second woman comes out. Much younger, dressed like the first, though her shawl (unfortunately, thinks Carlos) is less transparent and wrapped more tightly. She joins the others, just as assured, with a bigger smile, white-toothed. The odds are even better for the Indians now. Three against four (not counting the driver, fast asleep). The atmosphere has changed again.

The American woman asks, "So they have more than one wife?"

Carlos translates.

The Indian tells him, "In the old days. But now we are Catholics. We cannot stay in the past. Only death parts us."

"And this young woman?"

"My daughter."

He translates. The American woman says, "But they shouldn't make her do this. Posing for tourists with them. So unnatural. She wants to be in Quito, wearing jeans, not stuck out here in the middle of nowhere. I guess it's fashionable for us to think, Oh, Indians, great, but God, how she must loathe their lifestyle."

There's a silence. She thinks of LaVerne's desert boots kicked off in their hallway in Indiana, sharp stones wedged in the soles. Stones damaging the parquet. LaVerne's face, tanned and closed.

Carlos doesn't know whether he's meant to translate her

words, and if so, whether he can. The American hands out notes grimly. The Indians take the money without embarrassment. The Englishman follows suit. Paying the wife he thinks of his own wife saying, "My travelling days are over." But paying the daughter he suddenly remembers the letter from his son, about a new girl he's met. He writes, *This could be the one*. He smiles at the daughter. There is a future, they will have reinforcements. There will be new Sunday mornings. The daughter smiles back, meeting his eyes.

The American notes this. He says, "For another thousand you can take her with you."

Something in his tone stops Carlos, heading for the taxi. The girl's black hair is soft, her cheeks very round and polished. He feels excited. He comes behind her and takes her hand, trying to place it in the American's. He tells him, "Hold her while the others take photographs." The Englishman looks disapproving, Carlos can't tell why. He thinks, You never can with the English. When his girlfriend's face would stiffen in just that way, she'd pretend it hadn't. He keeps trying to join the girl to the American. Her hand is very small and firm. He calls to the others, "Have your cameras ready." And from his list of Useful Colloquialisms: "To snap them."

The Americans look at the brown earth, the Englishman at the treetops. No-one moves.

Whole

Monday. Why am I in Brazil? Because when my husband left me I sold my share of the furniture and came. I was numb, couldn't feel myself. Had to prove I could move, wasn't stuck forever in a half-empty flat in Southsea.

Manaus is like Southsea, ha ha. The kind of place where you think, Why am I here? Past its prime. Expensive — that's why my money's running out. Instead of the funfair, the opera house; equally vulgar, a giant pink and white cake with green, blue and yellow icing. Instead of ice-cream stalls, machines that squeeze juice from sugar-cane. Instead of the Solent with its sea-forts, the Rio Negro with its island petrol stations. Becoming, instead of the Channel, the Amazon. And all round, a horizon of what look like giant broccoli.

Down among them, unknown people I'll never meet.

Tuesday. Correction. I've met one. On the usual drag from lift to room, thinking as usual, Make an effort, organise money, I passed a man on a chair. Pale, knobbly features, loose mouth, stubble. He took me in, head to foot then middle. I felt like something in the meat-market by the docks, where they throw offal behind the wall. He said something in Portuguese.

I said, "*Não compreendo.*"

He tried English. "I am Antônio. You have a drink with me."

The dregs of male conversation. I walked away.

He called, "I show you something."

"Thanks, I've seen one."

He unlocked the door behind him and pointed. "You see nothing like that."

That's the trouble with going off alone. You lose heart and end up desperate for attention. I peered in. It was the bed he was pointing at, but there was someone in it, and Antônio was beckoning like some sideshow operator. So I'd be asked to pay. It was my wallet he fancied, not me.

I thought of all the coffee I drank in the bank while they phoned my credit card firm. No funds. Guess who diverted the payments. They gave me the name of a Lebanese moneychanger. That was too much, too threatening, as if the whole world's got stirred up and mashed together. Besides, I've no stomach for haggling. So I moved to this hotel. Not cheap, but cheaper.

Antônio wanted the door shut, but I refused unless he lent me the key. I approached the bed. A face looked up, chubby, copper-brown, with blue-black hair streaked orange. There were violet zigzags painted on the cheeks. The lips were full, the eyes black, deep-set and liquid but somehow dead, expressionless.

Watching my face intently, Antônio drew back the sheet. My God, a basket case. Naked, the arms and legs brief stumps. The skin of his chest and belly was taut and supple, mahogany colour. He smelt of strange oils, plant essences, like some exotic salad. I turned away, trying not to cry. Antônio grinned.

When I asked what happened he gave me a sly look.

"All right, how did he get here?"

I could see he was torn between keeping quiet and showing off. He made a pouncing movement. "We take." He waved at the flat horizon outside, eastward. "From far, many days."

"You abducted him?"

112

He didn't understand. I said hotly, "I'll tell the police," and he laughed in my face, his breath charged with stale tobacco and coffee. A pause.

He said, "Lady. Look."

I turned to look, reluctantly. He bent over the Indian, who'd been gazing at me, and spoke an unfamiliar language. The Indian turned his head away. I asked Antônio whether the language was Guaraní. He shook his head and sneered, as if to say, You're out of your depth. I asked what he'd said.

"I speak, foreign lady think him horrible. Bad. Kiss alligator before him."

Disgusted, I headed for the door — then paused, thinking of my empty room.

Antônio said, "Lady, look now."

He was almost pleading, like a child showing off a drawing. I went to look. The Indian's eyes were shut as if in pain, and I suddenly thought he was dying. His lips had contracted like a corpse's, exposing his teeth. Antonio's ragbag face was creased with delight.

He said, "Soon, lips gone."

"No! But how?"

He suddenly became cagey, nervous, eyeing the door. He said, "*Patrão* come soon. You go. Later, I come your room."

So, not money. "Stay away from my bloody room."

I went out. I'm scared to go back to the hotel. My brain's gone, my head's empty of ideas, except maybe to drink myself legless. I'm wandering by the great oily pontoon that floats up and down, watching the moored boats with their wide flat roofs and rows of hammocks. To escape to the mouth of the Amazon would cost more than I've got.

Wednesday. The Indian's with me.

Last night I got back late. Sitting in the corridor was a

different man; tall, black, who eyed me coldly. In the Indian's room I heard men laughing, laughter with an edge of malice and hysteria. Trying to sleep, with the choice of a muck-sweat or the air-conditioner rattling, I thought again of the police, but pictured the laughing men sounding plausible while I wrestled with Portuguese. My memory of the Indian was confused. Full lips, or the shrunken mouth of a corpse? And why had they pounced on him, what use was he to them? The humid room went round and round. I dragged myself off the bed and staggered to the door.

In the corridor was Antônio, dozing. Beside him a bottle of cane brandy. The click of my door must have roused him; he stumbled to his feet and moved away. I tiptoed down and heard him in the bathroom peeing like a horse. He'd left his keys.

I took them, and in a trance moved chair and bottle one door along. I unlocked the Indian's room. Blood pounded in my head as I heard Antônio's feet. Ah! They stopped one door away. I heard him plonk down. I went to the bed.

The Indian's eyes reflected the faint rectangle of window. Wide with terror? No, sad, unbelievably sad. Mouth like a drawstring, no lips at all. I made a decision. I rolled him in the sheet and picked him up, light as a child. Outside, one door away, Antônio dozed. I turned the key and carried the Indian to my room.

There I unwrapped him. His polished skin was perfect. But this was a woman, not a man. Wasn't it? He saw where I was looking and his eyes filled with tears. I cried too, for him, whatever they'd done to him, his exile in this unreal place, and for myself, my exile, my money crisis, wasted career, useless husband, rotten life. For the bits of myself I left behind in half a dozen cities.

My tears fell on him and the bed like rain. He stopped

114

crying and watched. I turned my head away. After a long time I went to the shower and wiped my face. When I came back I suddenly felt dizzy. My eyes were faulty. His lips were full and covered his teeth. He must have moved a little (the stumps of his arms were longer than I remembered) because I saw this *was* a man. His maleness was so small it must have been hidden.

I gave him a drink—he was desperately thirsty—and stroked his face. He smiled the most wonderful slow smile, bunching the zigzags on his cheeks. Something brushed my arm: the stump of his elbow. I didn't pull back, but somehow accepted it. I felt the rich skin of his chest, painted with strange markings, and said, "Oh, if I spoke your language! If I could take you home!"

He replied in his language. I nodded as if I understood. And here we are. What the hell can I do? Other than stroke him? His legs must have been so strong; the muscles down to the knee stumps are corded and supple. And now I see I was mistaken, his maleness is normal, more than normal. I must be smiling, because he's trying to raise himself on his elbows. With such hope and longing I'm just melting.

Thursday. At dawn, a thundering on my door. I phoned reception. No answer. The door splintered and in shot Antônio, then the tall black guy. They searched my room.

"*Onde fica?*"

I said, "*Não compre—*"

"Where is he? Martinho and me smell your cheap perfume in his room."

I won't dwell on Antônio and Martinho's other insults. I've heard them before, but these men are experts, even in a language not their own. For cutting people down to size they leave my husband in the shade.

I shouted, "You can abduct an Indian unpunished, but not me." I lied, "I've phoned Interpol with your descriptions."

Antônio drew a knife and I suddenly felt sick, but Martinho took it off him.

He said, "Lady, the Indio big money."

"How?"

"Sideshow in Rio. Maybe private circus. This people who lose parts when you make them feel bad, very rare."

"And how much of him would be left, by the time you got to Rio? Nothing, the way you treated him."

I wanted to ask who the Indian's people were, but knew I'd get no answer. I'm left with imagining them. So careful and caring, so delicate with each other's feelings. Watching their own feelings rise, to catch them before they turn into cruel words.

So how did my friend lay himself open to capture? Say, on shore making a dugout canoe. A chip of wood hits the eye of his brother, who gives him a tongue-lashing. My friend falls into the dugout, which slides into the water. Suddenly handless, he drifts downstream. More and more helpless till I restore him.

Today before dawn I made a decision. I'll take him home, whatever it takes. Now I've shamed Antônio and Martinho into going to face their boss empty-handed, I'll use the dregs of my money for a boat. I've drifted in this town; pathetic, waiting. Forgetting that after all the failures, reverses, insults, I'm still whole. All the bits work. And when I get back I'll go and drink coffee with the Lebanese.

Doing It

Bet you can't answer a simple question. How many moons has Mars got? Thought you wouldn't know. Here's a clue. How many eyes have you got?

That was good, wasn't it? I like asking questions. But now I'm here I don't see many people to ask. Ha ha. You're meant to laugh. I don't *see* anyone, do I?

Want another? What are the moons called? Dad couldn't answer either.

"Dad, what are the moons of Mars called?"

"Dot and Carrie."

Ha ha. I said, "I have told you."

"And I've told you to make that phone call."

"What phone call?"

He said, "Don't think I'll do it for you."

I remember loads of things he said. "I won't be here all your life." I wrote that down. "What will you do when I'm not here?" I wrote that down too. Here it is. When I feel these dots I think of his hands. He had warts on his hands. Well, he had when I was eight. Maybe the warts went, I don't know. He hasn't any now. Ha ha. Joke. He hasn't any hands.

I said, "The moons of Mars are Phobos and Deimos."

"Who told you that?"

"Bruce Forsyth."

"Very funny."

He did the tea at the day centre, Bruce Forsyth. All right,

that's who he sounded like. His breath smelt of extra-strong mints. He read it out of a library book I'd asked for.

"Phobos is an ellipsoid seventeen miles long, fourteen wide, and twelve high. Can you remember that, Alan?"

Could I remember! I asked what an ellipsoid is but he didn't know.

Dad didn't know either. He said, "They won't ask that at an interview."

"Ha ha, what interview?"

"It's not funny. There's a policy for people like you. You can get a job with the Council instead of wasting time on rubbish."

He didn't ask why I was laughing. I was laughing at the mayor asking, 'Now Alan, what are the measurements of Phobos?'

He said, "After all, you can answer a phone."

"Except when you leave a chair in the way."

"Put people through to the Council. Connect them."

"I don't want to connect anyone."

He said, "You're always phoning. Who were you on to this morning?"

"Sue Perkins."

"If I want jokes I'll turn the telly on."

Sue Perkins — that's who she sounds like — is in the reference library. I used to talk to her a lot. I can't phone from here. I have to make do with what I can remember.

Phobos crosses the Martian sky in only four and a half hours.

The Martian satellites may be captured asteroids.

I'd like to capture Deimos. Imagine it brought here. Go on, try. Lying outside … I was going to say, our house. Lying outside the town hall. Six miles high, ten long, seven and a half wide. Covered in dust and grooves and craters. It'd sink in quite a bit. They'd have to re-route the buses. Move the day centre. Not that that matters now.

'I won't be here all your life.'

I was terrified last night. Someone came in, his shoes creaked, he smelt of smoke. It was Dad. Ha ha, I thought it was. Hard and brittle with bits flaking off.

I said, "Go away."

He put his hand on my shoulder, so it wasn't Dad. He gripped hard.

I said, "Gerroff."

He said, "Someone's overexcited."

It was Michael Gove.

I tried to pinch his hand but he kept taking it away and putting it back, playing a game, not letting me. I could hear his metal watch strap.

He said, "So you're the culprit."

"What's a culprit?"

He just laughed. What *is* a culprit? I'd ask Bruce Forsyth, but I never meet him now.

Dad came in the kitchen. I was making a model, you can't guess what. Wrong! The other one, Deimos.

He said, "You'd be better off making baskets."

He didn't ask what the model was. Maybe it was that accurate he could tell it was Deimos at half an inch to the mile.

He said, "Instead of wasting your time."

The model got lost then. I threw it at him.

He said, "A bloody good thing you can't see. Or I'd show you the look on your face."

I got up in the night. I could tell it was night by the quiet traffic. You can't tell here, night and day are the same. I found the model under a chair but it hadn't gone hard. How do you make a model of a moon of Mars? Get a potato the right size, put papier-mâché over it. The papier-mâché dries hard like rock. Because that's all the moons are, big rocks.

I like rocks. When I was five Dad took me to the sea and I held a pebble. It was smooth but after a bit you noticed little pits. The sea made the other pebbles go, 'Sssh, sss'.

I tried putting the model in the oven. When it warmed up the oven smelt of stale mackerel. I kept checking but the model wouldn't go hard. Dad was asleep upstairs. I found his lighter fuel and poured it on. It took me ages to find his matches. When I tried to light it the fuel had dried so I put loads more on.

Michael Gove said, "Alan the arsonist," and I lashed out but he must have backed away because my hand just grazed the buttons on his cardigan. He laughed. What's an arsonist?

"You won't be asked to identify your father." A woman told me that afterwards. She didn't sound like anyone. I said it didn't matter not seeing, I'd know Dad by his smell.

She said, "Dead people smell different."

Crisp like burnt toast. She wouldn't let me near to touch him. Even though I hadn't touched him since I was eight.

'What will you do when I'm not here?' I'm doing it.

Theory & Design
in the Age of Innocence

We walked to a tree. The sun through its leaves and branches was warm on my skin. We looked at one of the things hanging on it.

"Right," he said, "find a name for that."

"The pehehehargorribololum."

Daddy sighed. "Isn't that a bit of a mouthful?"

I laughed. 'A bit of a mouthful' was a good joke, because the thing hanging there was tasty. I'd tried one and it was sweet and juicy with a small end you could bite to get started.

He said, "You don't want to say all that each time you refer to it."

"Why not? Who would I refer to it *to*?"

He smiled — at least I think he did, because I could only look with my eyes half shut.

"To me of course. Or to yourself, to help you think about it."

"Well how about just the pehehehar?"

"I might think you were laughing."

"Just pehar, then," I grumbled. "Or even pear."

"Pear sounds fine."

Daddy moved away and I followed, protesting.

"Where are we going? We haven't finished that tree yet. There are lots of things on it."

"Yes, and they're all pehars. Pears rather. The one we've just looked at isn't *the* pear, it's *a* pear."

I pulled a face. I was getting a headache.

"What if I want to refer to that one?"

I pointed to the fruit at the very top.

"You say, 'The pear at the top of the tree.'"

"You've just said '*the* pear.' You said we had to say '*a* pear.'" I looked longingly at the treetop. "Can't I call that one the phlegorog?"

Daddy sighed again. The leaves all around us stirred.

"It's not worth giving them individual names. They don't last long enough. If you don't pick that one soon it'll fall off and rot, and those stripy things you haven't named yet will eat it." He looked at me with a frown—I think it was a frown. "Look, talking of stripy things, why don't we leave fruit and name an insect?"

"Fine by me."

We walked—I walked, he sort of glided—to a clearing, past trees loaded with the things that only yesterday I decided to call mangoes, bananas, and figs. On the grass under the fig tree was a creature with big back legs, the knees back to front.

I said, "Spregglygoggorus."

"Sheer cacophony, pathetic," he spat, showering me with a tropical storm of saliva. "Find something euphonious."

I pretended to understand. "All right, cackledeflumius."

"Please! Look, an arbitrary relationship between signifier and signified doesn't work well. Just name things for what they *do*."

"But I want to be original."

"Originality is overrated," he said, with some bitterness, I thought.

The thing jumped.

"All right, grassleaper."

He grunted. "I don't like that *s* to *l* transition."

"Not euphonious," I sneered.

"Just bloody awkward."

"All right, grass*hopper*. Even though it doesn't hop."

He nodded. "Sometimes sound takes precedence over sense."

We walked on into a clearing. There were two big beasts with clumsy-looking feet, sarcastic expressions, and humps.

"Did you design these, Daddy?" (I didn't say I thought they were a disaster.)

"Who else? You think I had help from a committee?"

He sounded so cross I didn't dare ask what a 'committee' was.

I said, "I suppose it's one name for both."

"Far more convenient. And please, think expressiveness. Think euphony."

"Camelammalamma."

He raised a huge eyebrow. "Expressive, yes. Euphonious to a degree. But a sign of the true artist is what he chooses to leave out."

I could tell which way the wind was blowing, "All right, camel."

"Good."

I studied the beasts. "They *aren't* the same," I objected. "One's got something hanging off its belly."

"Yes. That's a he-camel. The other's a she-camel."

Just then the thing on the he-camel started to grow. It stretched and stretched until I thought it might burst. Suddenly the he-camel put his front legs on the back of the other camel and made the thing disappear. He made very strange movements. My skin began to feel hot, and my willy very heavy. I looked down and saw I was stretched to bursting just like the camel.

"What are we to do with you?" Daddy asked.

"I don't know," I moaned.

"Hmm. It occurs to me that you're the only creature without a mate." He sighed. "I'll see what I can do."

Next morning I was eating a pear—still annoyed because I preferred pehehehar—when Daddy called me. I found him looking at a heap of wool and bone, the remains of a sheep. They seem to die easily.

He said, "Adam, I'm going to make you a mate."

"Out of that lot? I thought you made me out of clay?"

He looked around as if someone else might be listening, glowing red like he does when he's cross. Or embarrassed.

"That's as may be. Do you want a mate or not?"

"Well it's not 'not'," I grumbled.

"Then watch."

He took some of the leg bones and stretched them. He squeezed the skull so it was nearly round, I'm not sure how. He did things to the other bones, then laid them all out in the dust, in a shape which I had to admit (feeling my own bones with my fingers) was pretty similar to mine. But I still wasn't optimistic about how she'd turn out.

Sensing my doubts, Daddy said, "This is *pragmatic* design. Using readily available materials as a starting point."

"Oh."

"Or you could call it *elementarist*."

I began to feel more confident. He obviously knew what he was doing.

"What's elementarist?"

"An element is a structural part that clearly registers in the composition. Preferably of simple geometric form."

"Great."

He pulled down some creeper, cleared the tough stems of leaves, and strung them along the bones.

"Now we have an armature. Right. You can help."

124

We went to a stream, where he told me to dig handfuls of soft mud from the bottom and put it into his cupped hands. As his hands are very much bigger than mine it took a long time.

"I'm tired," I said.

"Is that what you'll say to your mate when she asks you to you-know-what?"

"No."

"No, so keep at it."

When we had enough we went back to the bones and he moulded the clay around them. I was so excited! It was beginning to look like a real creature. I wasn't sure whether it looked like me, so I went to a still pool to check my reflection. I nearly fell in.

When I got back she was standing up. He was just giving her hair, from the wool from the dead sheep. He put plenty on her head, and quite a lot on her lower belly. I wasn't sure about the body hair.

"What's that for?"

"Ornament. You've got hair there, haven't you?"

"Not as much as that."

He looked offended. "Ornament isn't a crime."

"It's all right, Daddy. I'm sure she'll be great."

I went close. She had eyes, a nose, and lips like mine, but—maybe my imagination—her face reminded me of a sheep. One of her eyes was bigger than the other.

"I know what you're thinking, Adam. You don't want too much symmetry. It has a deadening effect."

"Right."

She was unlike me in having two big lumps on her chest. They were different sizes—to match her eyes, I supposed. Daddy smiled, at least I think he did; when he's glowing I can never tell.

"I made those with implants of that fruit." (What I later called melon.) "Do you like them, Adam? When you get to know her you can fondle them. Right, take her away. Oh — you might like to name her first."

"Unaroonakaboona," I offered.

Daddy raised a sardonic eyebrow.

"All right, just Una." To her I said, "Hello, Una."

"Uechch."

She sounded like one of those jumping things in ponds. (Must remember — I still haven't named those.)

"Shall we go for a walk?"

"Uh-eech."

I took her hand and off we went, Daddy watching us proudly.

The sun was going down when we got back. Daddy was lying in the clearing dozing, glowing deep purple. He heard the rustle of leaves as we approached, sat up, and smiled down on us.

"I was tired after all that effort. Well son, how did it go?"

"It didn't. For one thing she doesn't walk right. She keeps falling over."

"Too much asymmetry, perhaps."

"And, she just makes noises unrelated to any meaning."

He looked thoughtful. "Too much reliance on language can lead one astray, you know."

"Maybe, but also she smells like rotting vegetation. I fondled her — she didn't seem to mind, at least all she said was, 'Wer wer' — but her skin feels like tree bark."

Daddy gave another deep sigh which shook the forest.

"I'm sure the concept is right. The fault must be in the execution. Oh well, back to the drawing-board."

"What's a drawing-board?"

"Never mind. Your descendants will find out. If you ever have any," he added darkly.

And off he went, crashing through the bushes. Descendants? What are they? As for Una, I haven't seen her around.

Daddy decided that because I'm such a good 'specimen', whatever that means, he'd try again using what he called *iconic* design.

"I'm going to model her directly onto you. Actually this may be canonic rather than iconic. Either way, here goes."

He told me to stand still and started fiddling around behind me.

"Ow, you're hurting."

He tut-tutted, told me to wait, and went into the bushes. He came back with a length of creeper dripping with sap and held it for me to drink from. Whatever it was, it made me feel good and I couldn't feel what he was up to at my back. All I was aware of was his shadow in the dust ahead of me, his hand busy with a knife and lumps of something—clay perhaps.

I must have dozed off standing up, because the next thing I knew Daddy was tapping me on the shoulder.

"Feel behind you," he said.

I put my hands behind my back. My back had gone further away! In fact my lower back felt more like a belly. It *was* a belly. A very smooth belly, not hairy like mine. I moved my hands further up. There was something sticking out which I could just about reach—*two* things sticking out. They felt very pleasant, soft but firm, but my shoulders hurt trying to get my arms up to them. I bent forward to see if that made it easier.

"Ow," said a voice. "My back." A musical voice, not gruff and booming like Daddy's, more like a bird singing.

"Who are you?" I asked.

"I haven't got a name."

Daddy came round and looked down at me, glowing gold, with a huge grin. He spread his hands as if to say, 'Sorted.' I wanted to call my new companion Deedledeedledurdur but thought better of it.

"I'd like to give you a long name," I said, "but Daddy only likes them short. So I'll call you Dee."

Dee and I spent quite a few days together. She was nice to talk to. When she wanted my attention she bumped the back of my head with hers. She noticed things around the place that I hadn't. 'Look at those birds gorging themselves on berries,' for example. Or after it had rained and the big leaves of the gunnera (as I later called it) were dripping, 'Listen. You can pick out a rhythm.'

When we walked around we had to agree who was going to walk backwards. We took turns watching camels, sheep, and other beasts mating. "I'd like to do that," she said. "Wouldn't you?"

"Yes."

But we couldn't. She could just about reach my willy, which was nice, especially as her hands were softer than mine, but it was harder for me to reach what she had instead. I tried bending and putting my hand between our legs, but she complained again about her back.

In the end we fell out. If she said, "You say such interesting things, Adam," I wasn't sure she wasn't being sarcastic because I couldn't see her face. When I did a poo she complained about the smell, and when she peed I got annoyed because she couldn't do it properly.

"It's no good," I said to Daddy one day. "I need to get her off my back."

"And him off mine," Dee added.

"Oh dear."

"What is iconic design anyway?" I asked.

"You use an existing artefact as a pattern and change one aspect. That's why I built her onto you."

"We can't watch the moon rise with our arms around each other," Dee complained. "I'm tired of taking turns to look at things. And we can't you-know-what like the camels."

Daddy sighed. "I'll do what I can."

One morning I woke with a start. My back and bottom seemed to be on fire. I felt behind me. My bottom had no cheeks! It was horribly flat.

Daddy turned up, glowing amber.

"Where's Dee?" I asked.

"Gone off. You wouldn't like the look of her, Adam. Her back's raw and she's got no bottom."

"Won't it grow back?"

Daddy looked embarrassed. "To be honest she doesn't like the look of you either, bottom or no bottom."

I later learned that, not believing we were the only couple on earth, she'd gone to search for another mate.

Weeks went by. My bum grew back. I kept asking Daddy when he was going to try again, but he just changed the subject, pointing out more plants and animals for me to name. He quibbled all the time, so it took ages. I wasn't getting any job satisfaction, or willy satisfaction for that matter. I kept remembering the feel of Dee's hands, and my hands on her belly, and feeling sad. Watching animals mate didn't excite me anymore. Also, I didn't see much of Daddy, and began to feel really lonely.

One evening, sitting by a waterfall watching the sunset through the banana leaves, I heard an unfamiliar voice, powerful and melodious. It scared me so much I hid among some rocks.

"Run along dear," it said. "Say hello. He won't bite. You-know-who tried to make him but couldn't get him up and running. I had to sort him out. Good luck."

None of it made sense. Whose was the voice? Who was it talking to? Had to sort me out—how? I sat hunched, waiting for whoever spoke to go away. After a minute or so there was a rustling in the undergrowth behind me, and then, amazingly, soft hands on my shoulders.

"Hello Adam," said a voice—a small voice, not the one I'd just heard, but just as melodious. More amazingly still, what felt like a warm belly was pressed against the back of my head.

"I'm supposed to introduce myself."

I was too scared to turn and look.

"What design are you? Pragmatic? Iconic?"

She laughed, which made her belly tickle my neck.

"So it's true about your upbringing. Oh well, Mummy told me to humour you."

"Who's Mummy?"

"Your Granny, actually. Which technically makes me your auntie, but let's leave consanguinity issues aside for now. I've heard you're good at names. Want to give me one?"

She sounded a bit clever for my liking so I thought I'd impress her with a long one, especially since Daddy wasn't around.

"We don't want too arbitrary a relationship between signified and signifier, do we? As it's evening I'll call you Eveningdescendsineden."

"Ridiculous. Find something shorter."

I thought, Got a mind of her own. Could be trouble. But I didn't care, because she leaned over me, long hair spilling over my shoulder. She smelt like blossom, with an undertone of something rich and exciting.

"What's that thing?" she asked. "A mushroom growing on you?"

She was right, it *was* growing.

Romey and Jullit

It is with a sense of both awe and fulfilment that the author submits the one hundred and ninety-ninth annual report of Project Random. The body of the report follows this brief introduction.

The author's enthusiasm is not intended as undue influence on the Committee. As in previous years the bulk of our subjects' output is of what has traditionally been called 'baseline quality', though the author prefers the word *bêtises*. A short extract from Text No. 5985/0393PY will suffice as an example:

38re9fdnmrck,.vc,.,.b,xsdislotrilundod.,nutfbibiuwk,fbv, mb\af[Ofk

Our world vocabulary database is of course being scanned for elements such as 'bibiuwk' and 'Ofk', but I think the Committee will agree that there is little here to advance our thesis.

Subject 6177 is but one among very many. Nevertheless, the past year has seen a sense of restrained excitement up and down our normally hushed and sober corridors, especially since the output can hardly be other than random. The subject, an Amazonian howler, is of lower intelligence than many of our other subjects (see table, Appendix One), and was born out of captivity. Initial domestication consisted of being tied by a long rope to the corner-post of a hut in which manioc was processed: not an ideal beginning. The subject is an assiduous worker, enjoying the simple rattle of the keyboard and the movement of the cursor across the screen, and (unlike Subject 6003) has not attempted to access and re-file sensitive project data. It is, nevertheless, too soon to reach a definitive analysis of the output, and the author here presents a mere summary.

Our attention was first drawn to this subject's output by Text No. 6I77/0693BG, titled (by the subject) RO, NJO. Although consisting almost entirely of *bêtises* this text, it was noted, had a similar length to the target text. The final lines read as follows:

RO. tomnvpk.,wel.,ansd?
JO. Methinks 'tis so.

Here the text ends. The subject became unnaturally excited, and the computer malfunctioned. A soft aromatic fruity substance was found jamming Drive A. Nevertheless, researchers felt a breakthrough had been achieved.

Texts Nos. 6177/0893EV and 6I77/0893XM soon followed, titled respectively RUM AND JOLT and RAM, EO, AND JRIORNSV. Each had a BI (*bêtise* index) of less than fifty per cent. However, the author prefers to move quickly on to Text No. 6177/0993ZQ. Here for the first time we are able to apply the language of literary criticism as well as that of statistical theory.

In this short and highly intelligible text, titled ROMM AND JULIE, recognisable elements of the target text abound. It consists entirely of one extended scene, in a room in the city of Vorn. As fighting is heard in the streets outside, two six-year-old children, Romm and Julie, are berated by their fathers, Mr Monty and Mr Calpott, for some unspecified crime. A sense of doom and guilt hangs over this scene. The children, egged on by a friend, McCuty, have conspired together, therefore their fathers (aided by various middle-aged uncles, priests, and nurses) will conspire to punish them. The scene ends inconclusively, with only the vaguest hints as to either crime or punishment, but with, if anything, an intensification of mood.

A further text, No. 6177/1093WW, made an even greater impression on the researchers. Titled ROMU ON J'JILLA, it is set in clearly recognisable *milieux*. (It is difficult, at this juncture, to remind oneself that one is dealing with purely random outcomes, and that any impression of an evolutionary process is spurious.) On first reading it was assumed that the title hinted at some sexual encounter, but the eponymous lovers of the title never meet.

Mist and haze dominate the piece. (140 references to 'mist' or its synonyms were recorded.) The characters are melancholy and unfulfilled. J'Jilla, a girl of twelve in Veroni, wanders the streets with her nurse, who tries to interest her in the Scalligger tombs, the bridge on the River Adage with its 'merillons', and the towering shape of the Castelvacuum. But J'Jilla is dreaming of marriage—not to County Harris, to whom she is betrothed, but a dim figure wearing 'armour like a lobster' and 'a mask with a horsehair moustache'.

Meanwhile, in the city of Edy, a young 'sammeree' warrior dreams as he rides along by the seashore. He imagines a young girl in a strange white flowing dress, whose singing in a strange language, and whose free, spontaneous dancing (so unlike the controlled movements of his city's 'gashers'), touch his heart. After a series of battles he ends up on a small island, stranded and wild.

Back in Veroni, marriage has failed to cure J'Jilla, who is eventually declared mad by her husband and locked in a tower on his country farm in the Venuto, from which she looks down at pigs and chickens, and out at the swirling mist on the horizon. The author's satisfaction in perusing this text (BI only 5.332 per cent) was somewhat tempered by the wistful sadness it (of course accidentally) conveyed.

Text No. 6177/1 193PP comes even closer to the target text. REMERE EN JELEET opens with an unfamiliar motif: Remere, a young man on horseback, is handed a cup of 'Eisenbräu' by a girl of sixteen, Jeleet. The location is not specified, only 'North', presumably Northern Italy. Remere's hand shakes as he takes the cup and some of the brew is spilt.[1]

The setting moves to the familiar balcony scene. Remere sings Jeleet a serenade expressing his desire for her. She throws down a flower with purple petals. The scene is inconclusive. Remere does not ascend to the balcony but at length drifts homeward, where (one presumes in his imagination) the scene is repeated, this time with an erotic outcome.

The final scene takes place in church as Jeleet is married to the County Pyrus. There are vague references to stained glass. In a strange anachronism, a greetings telegram of many pages is received from Remere, now 'across the sea', justifying at length his actions in the two previous scenes. The style of this document is excessively cerebral, and all dramatic interest is thrown away by this turgid intrusion. The piece ends before we are told of Jeleet's reaction.

Average word length in the 'telegram passage' is 11.732, and required reading age would be 17 years 3.2 months. In a human subject one would be able to state unequivocally that this degree of complexity represented a major step. In the case

---

[1] The appearance here of a German word emphasised for the research team one striking property of the subject's output: that nearly all legible text is English. The statistical implications are being investigated.

of Subject 6177 it is, of course, spurious to attribute developmental qualities to what, according to our thesis, is an entirely random process. Nevertheless, it was necessary to issue a firm reminder on this point to all research staff, including temporaries and part-timers.

This brings the author to the final and most recent text dealt with in this report, No. 6177/0194AA. The title is ROMEY AND JULLIT. Length is almost identical to that of the target text, being shorter by a factor of 0.9999346. BI is low at 3.73 per cent. The output may be summarised as follows.

Although the opening scenes are close to those of the target text, the fight scenes between Monandrogues and Copulets have a dreamy, insubstantial quality. Furthermore, there are strange intrusions from related (non-target) texts. For instance, reference to one meeting 'upon the heath' and to another 'or here, or at the Capitol'. In a further scene Romey, from the balcony (for here the setting is his own apartment), soliloquises that he loves Jullit 'not wisely but too well'. Jullit appears, he lets down a ladder and she climbs to the balcony. Unity of time is observed as the couple consummate their love offstage, interest onstage being provided by the unlikely entrance of peasants in festive attire, who perform a dance.

Jullit opens the shutters to the morning sun exclaiming, 'if that be love, me-thinks love be o'erpraised'. It soon appears, however, that she is with child. The opposition of the two families is strangely muted in this version, and the couple choose a home. In this passage elements of J'Jilla's tour of the city from ROMU ON J'JILLA are re-used, or, one should rather say, coincidentally reappear, with Romey rather than the Nurse as her interlocutor.

The text now diverges even more from the target text. In a scene with Jullit's Nurse, Romey expresses restlessness and dissatisfaction with married life. The Nurse seduces him. Jullit learns of this betrayal with understandable horror, and in her distress turns for advice to her old friend and counsellor Mr Lawrance, a former priest. He in turn seduces her.

A series of street fights now ensues, but in this version it is Romey and Jullit who head the opposing factions. The older generation side with Jullit, the younger with Romey. When his friend Meriticio is killed Romey loses heart for the fight and sues for peace. The Nurse commits suicide; Mr Lawrance is exiled.

One is tempted to say that the final scene 'fails to learn the lessons of the dramatic failure of the end of REMERE EN JELEET', but to talk in such terms is, of course, nonsensical. The scene in question consists of an intimate, extended, rambling, and dramatically inconclusive dialogue between Romey and Jullit, interspersed with scenes of what can only be described as sexual experimentation: impossible to stage, in the unlikely event that one would wish to do so.

The text concludes with what has presented the research team with something of a dilemma: a series of *bêtises* presented as dialogue. A colleague has suggested that these are 'intended as animal grunts'. It was of course pointed out that to present the possibility of a creature such as Subject 6177 exhibiting 'intention' (other than that of achieving the basic satisfaction of rattling keys) is mere anthropocentrism. Nevertheless, the author apologises in advance should any such tone appear to have affected the above summary, and assures the Committee that the apparent use of the language of dramatic criticism is used merely to illuminate the character of the text.

Full copies of all texts are available on request. Appendices will be found towards the end of the report. A photograph of the author together with Subject 6177 appears on the inside back cover.

The Fan

She had caught him out in an affair, and now they were starting again. They walked through the woods talking of travel. The woods were a tame strip between houses and a golf course, and down by the brook, where new sewers had been laid, new saplings were just beginning to add height.

She said, "We could go to Canada for a year. You could work there."

She thought it would be a relief to be far from the other woman. Even now the woman's husband would phone her to ask angrily why she hadn't prevented it. She tried to explain that she and her husband had no authority over one another, that she could never be sure what he was thinking.

She repeated, "Do you fancy Canada?"

He thought of the song *The Green Fields of Canada*, the young Irishman's farewell to his home, and a tear came into his eye. He wiped it away hastily, as if it were an insect, so she wouldn't notice. He said, "Possibly. I thought of somewhere more exotic."

"Where?"

He didn't know. Somewhere with stars he could lie and look at, without street lights. Where he could lose himself in a profound blackness, the earth warm under him. A desert perhaps. He knew if he said this his wife would say, "All right, a desert," and he'd have to list possible names, consult the atlas. So he said nothing.

She said, not one to give up easily, "Canada's interesting."

"But what would you do?"

"Get some kind of job. Anything. The children could easily go to school there."

They walked in silence for a while. Over their heads a squirrel leapt from one tree to another, showering ash keys. She took his hand and rubbed it, as if trying to bring him back to life. Since he gave up the other woman he'd been empty of feeling. She too was empty now, her anger all burned out. She held his hand against her hip as they walked, and he felt a quiver of desire, as if his skin ached. He would have liked them to slither halfway down to the brook and make love among the rhododendrons, but he feared she'd ask whether he'd been here with the other woman. He had not. They walked on.

She asked, "What do you think?"

"I'd really imagined going abroad alone."

She kept hold of his hand because that had become part of the rhythm of the walk, but her chest and stomach felt suddenly cold, encapsulated, as if she were a vacuum flask.

He never expected the affair to work. He knew it was doomed, that there would be much more pain than pleasure. But without pain there would be no art, no *Tosca*, no *Tristan and Isolde*. He'd read only weeks before, as if fate were preparing him for the encounter, about the 'unassailable soul of the warrior', and elsewhere, about following love whenever called, 'even though you know he will wound you'. When he stood in the school orchestra pit that smelt of old timber and dust, and the woman, sewing in the wings, looked down at him with smouldering eyes, he could not deny himself to her.

He was conducting his Opus Three, *Overture and Incidental Music to The Real King Arthur*. The play, comparing history with legend, had been written by his daughter's English teacher. The woman, whose children were also at the high school, had designed the costumes.

Biting a thread, she joked, "Only Opus Three? At your age?"

"I'm a late starter."

"Well at least you won't peak too early."

He found that his daughter considered her smarmy and overbearing. By this time they were starting the affair, and as his daughter suspected nothing he thought it tactically wise to agree.

The affair was brief. His wife was more perceptive than he'd realised. He thought she'd fail to notice his extra hours at rehearsal, and he was right. But he hadn't allowed for her noticing his erratic changes of mood, the hours he sat dreamily at the piano. In the messy aftermath, his wife and the woman's husband picked through the rubble like fire investigators. The woman asked him to pretend to give her up but go on seeing her in secret. He refused. He also refused to hide from his wife the fact that she still phoned him. The woman cried, but respected him. But when she heard of his daughter's remark, and his full agreement with it, she felt betrayed and her respect evaporated. She wrote to say she detested him, his way of life, and most of all, his music.

She receded into his past, a ghost he sometimes saw when the coach returned their children from school trips. The pain from such sightings, from the knowledge of what she now thought of him, he bore almost with pride. He'd prepared for the worst. He had the unassailable soul of the warrior. Besides, the suffering would feed his art. The woman was his Mathilde Wesendonck, his wife was his Cosima. Of course, the comparison with Wagner was inexact. For example, Wagner would have scorned the school orchestra pit as acoustically disastrous.

What was harder to bear was his wife's pain. The way she scraped and scraped at the wood of cupboards for hours to strip them, then collapsed into a chair, too drained even to watch TV or put on music. It was a dull, uninspiring stoicism. He preferred the blazing anger she'd shown when she first found out and they fought like animals, she tearing at his face and lunging at his testicles, he pinning her wrists and roaring at her. These encounters would often end with their pulling each other's clothes off and making love with intense relief. But when, soon after the walk in the woods, a kind of fog came down between them, he felt oppressed by their life. There was nothing noble about it. Their quarrels were trivial, about spilt jam, socks the children lost.

In the library of the college where he worked was a handbook of the world's higher education. He began to browse in it after work, and write letters asking for one-year appointments. His wife, who in the past had not noticed discrepancies in his timing, now thought he might be seeing the woman again. She wondered how to be sure. He seemed withdrawn and preoccupied, but that could be work, or her own shut-down state. It wasn't in her to spy, go through his pockets, or wait and watch, on her days off, in the café across the road from his department. Besides, she'd rather live with uncertainty than know the answer, because if the answer was Yes, it would be the end.

Nevertheless, she couldn't help commenting on his lateness. He said, "I'm just spending time in the library."

"Doing what?"

He was unwilling to tell her about the applications. If they came to nothing he'd feel small in her eyes. "Research."

"On what?" Not meaning to test him now, simply wanting to be reassured that they could still talk. About anything, the more down-to-earth the better. If he wanted to let off steam about work, that was fine, then she could do the same. Except that there was no steam inside her, only ice. She smiled wryly at the image, his steam melting her ice.

He asked, "What are you smiling at? Don't you believe me? I'm researching the life of Wagner." He thought that a convenient subject, since he already knew so much, and she wasn't aware how much he knew.

She said, "Tell me about it." She thought, Tell me anything, anything you think or feel.

He told her Wagner's life was like a fairytale: nearly drowned at sea escaping from a dull routine, dogged by failure in Paris, never losing faith in his vision, rescued at last from poverty by King Ludwig of Bavaria. Soothed by Cosima. He omitted any mention of Mathilde.

She asked, "And what will you compose next? What's Opus Four?"

He shrugged. He distrusted the subject. He had some disjointed themes in his head, which he would have liked to play to get her reaction, but he feared they would skip back into discussing Opus Three, inseparable from the school play and the other woman. She might ask again, as she'd asked so often, "But why? Why did you do it?" And when he failed to reply, "Admit it, I bored you, you wanted to fuck somebody different, a different body." Making him seem crude and self-seeking. Not someone who simply gave of himself. Not someone prepared to pluck the *Heidenröslein* and be lacerated with thorns.

He received a letter from the University of Omdurman. Yes, they would employ him for a year, to develop a course in acoustics, the physics of music, the mathematics of harmony. The name Omdurman excited him. The scene of the last cavalry charge, in which the youthful Winston Churchill had taken part. A city of traders in gold, at the meeting of two great rivers. He brought the letter home, smiling.

His wife said, "I didn't know you were writing letters."

He played down his having applied, and spoke enthusiastically about his head of department's web of foreign contacts. His wife was left with the impression that he hadn't so much sought this offer as had it thrust upon him. She knew nothing of Omdurman. They looked at the map together. Her husband seemed to know what it would be like there, tracing the two rivers with his finger, the finger that had secretly touched the other woman. But she received no impression except, from the climate graph, one of heat.

She said, "Good. When do we go?"

She thought he seemed surprised by her willingness.

"July."

The University had enclosed some fact sheets, which didn't seem to interest her husband. She went through them carefully, trying to decide what clothes to take, what injections were needed, where the children would go to school. She asked him to check how much of his salary he would be able to send home, and at what rate of exchange. They could let the house for a year, but the rest might only just cover the mortgage, and they had other payments to keep up.

The more she read about education, the more uneasy she became. There were only Islamic schools, and one private college run by Jesuit priests. The older child was about to choose her GCSE subjects, the younger was struggling with his maths. She wanted them to be happy, to have successful lives. They weren't too happy now because of the emotional fog inside their home, but at least they could look forward to careers and supportive partners.

She said, "I don't think we can go."

Her husband stared at her, his mouth trying to form a reply.

She explained at length about education. He went for a long walk, looking all round him at the fields, at the distant houses and still more distant hills, as if for something he'd lost. When he returned it was dark. The stars were obscured by cloud. The children were going through their bedtime rituals, which absorbed all his wife's attention. When they'd settled they looked at one another, each trying to read the other's face.

She said, "Perhaps you should go."

His heart leapt. He said, "Without you? No."

"But it's what you wanted."

"When I said that ..." He shrugged. He'd been about to continue, 'I was confused', but that would have been a gross lie. The pain had given him a sense of clarity, of living deeply. It was now, when the pain had dulled, that he felt confused. He said, "I don't know, I don't know."

In the end he decided to go. It would enliven his CV. It could even be a good career move. The music of another continent could inspire and inform his Opus Four. In the desert, away from street lights, he'd see more stars than he'd believed possible. As for money, he'd be able to send a proportion home: he'd checked that with the consulate. The exchange rate was poor, and of course his UK salary would be suspended, but his wife assured him that she'd manage. There was just enough, and it was only for a year. Meanwhile the University would pay for one return flight home, and one return flight for his family to Omdurman. After he'd settled in, they'd come for a few weeks' holiday.

The night before he was to leave, in bed, his wife cried. She realised she hadn't quite believed he would go alone. She went over the past few years and thought how things ought to have been. She thought how other families, their friends, lingered over meals together, played ball games in their gardens. Her husband asked what was wrong.

145

"I feel abandoned."

He said, "I could still not go." He wondered whether, if she leapt at this, he'd feel frustration or relief.

"Your decision's made. I wouldn't respect you now if you didn't go."

He dabbed at her tears, trying not to cry himself. The books he'd read before his affair, about the path of the warrior, about love, hadn't mentioned this kind of situation. He felt his resolve in danger. For months the fog had stopped his wife's words and feelings touching him deeply. Later when she fell asleep he looked at her face, which suddenly looked unfamiliar. When next he saw her she would look even more strange. He sought for a form of words that would carry him through. He thought, This is what I wanted. No, what I'm fated to do. The thoughts made him feel no different. He hummed to himself the Prelude to Act One of *Lohengrin*. The music warmed his heart, and after a while he too slept.

The journey to London seemed ordinary. The train, the scenery were pleasantly familiar. The idea that he was taking a flight alone seemed unreal. When he'd flown before it had always been with his wife and children on holidays, or on rare academic trips with colleagues. It was only when he got off the Tube that he felt his real journey begin. He was staying with friends who lived half a mile from the Tube station, too close for it to be worth taking a cab. He moved his four heavy pieces of luggage two at a time, walking ten paces with the first two, going back for the second two, walking forward till all four pieces were reunited, then repeating the process. Sweating freely, he submitted himself to the discipline. He noticed that when his luggage was at its greatest separation, he felt anxious, but that the anxiety diminished as it came back together.

In the morning, once again, it was hard to believe he was going. His friends usually drove him to Euston for a train home. When they drove to Heathrow he almost called out that they'd taken a wrong turning. But at the airport he was reassured, because by the check-in desk were the most handsome people he'd ever seen. Three men, very tall, with high domed foreheads and finely sculptured faces, their skin a rich, slightly dusty black. On their wiry night-black hair sat delicate round skullcaps of white openwork. Two women, wide-eyed, attractive, their heads covered by white shawls of surprising delicacy and lightness. His heart lifted on seeing them. It was clear he was taking the right step, going to a land of people such as these.

Walking to the plane he had a moment of doubt. There were other aircraft, from India, the Far East, Australasia. Was he going to the right continent after all? Was it possible that his destiny lay elsewhere, that he'd somehow misread the signals? But here were the steps, his feet were leaving the surface of his homeland, now visible either side of the handrail, grey, crisscrossed by tubes and cables.

His was a middle seat, facing a pale grey bulkhead with a mural of flying storks. In the window seat on his right was another of the men with fine black features, but rather smaller and slighter. In the aisle seat, a bulky man who greeted him.

"Hi there. They don't give us a hell of a lot of space."

They smiled at one another. He wondered whether he should have perhaps gone to America. The fellow was so relaxed and confident. The man by the window was more formal. He seemed to have no English. They nodded politely to one another. Well, soon he'd be able to address these people in their own tongue. After the first meal was cleared away, against the steady throb of the engines, he studied the language book.

147

The poor man, where is his house? — Sir, I do not know.
Is the road long? — Yes, the road is very long indeed.
O girl, mother of big earrings —

He closed the book. He would not be speaking to women, not socially, not alone. To go through the pain of abandoning the other woman, only to fall into the same trap in Omdurman through sheer loneliness, would be a cosmic joke.

He closed his eyes and put on the headphones; alien music filtered through him washing away the past. A new beginning, a new beginning. The singer's voice hesitated and soared in quarter-tones, and a flock of string instruments, like a flock of evening swifts, hesitated and soared with him, while a drum like a sleeper's pulse beat gently and artfully. He settled into his seat. Perhaps this new stream would flow into his own compositions. As Wagner had transcended the narrow rivalries of German and Italian opera, had forged a new whole on the anvil of his suffering, he would bring Omdurman home, or home to Omdurman.

A journey of peace — And you Sir, God give you peace.

He dozed as the plane beat southwards.

When drinks came the American asked where he was headed. He explained about the University. The American said every rainy season some part of the one railroad from port to capital was washed away, blocking the flow of food and raw material. "That's when they turn to air freight. Which is where I come in."

With his big face and wide shoulders, the man had the air of someone not very important in his own right, but useful as part of a greater whole. Another voice in the chorus, two more hands to the pump. He kept twisting in his seat.

"My goddamn back. Injured it years ago."

"So what do you do on long flights?"

The man grinned. "Suffer, what else? In the hotel I run a bath, hot as I dare, and lower myself in. Fwsssh! And you? Which hotel are you in?"

"Don't know yet. Being met, by the University."

Later, after crossing a new coastline, he spoke to the man on his right.

"Where are you going?"

"El Obeid."

"What is it like, El Obeid?"

"It is my home."

They smiled, and again nodded politely. Beyond the man's shoulder, through the window, the sunset was a fiery brushstroke on the horizon. He thought, The lone and level sands stretch far away, and spent a dreamy half hour trying vainly to remember where the line came from. At least now he could write to his wife and children: *I watched the sun set behind the desert*. The brushstroke faded. Night fell.

When the aircraft rolled to a halt he felt tense until the doors were opened. The air outside had a burnt smell, like clods of couch-grass on a slow bonfire. He filled in an immigration form on poor quality paper, irritated by the delay, then filed past a control kiosk. A man with stars on his shoulder-straps took the form and stamped his passport. The man's face, dark brown rather than black, was pitted as if from smallpox. He went through, found his luggage, all four pieces intact, and pressed on to the arrivals hall.

He stood on tiptoe, looking above the crowd for a placard bearing his name. He felt that once he saw it, in this echoing space, something would have been proved, something settled. It was like a photographic negative of the departure lounge. Now he and the other Europeans were the exotic

149

ones, weaving in and out of the crowd of black men like figures from someone's dream. There was no sign of the tall fine-looking men and handsome women he'd seen at the check-in. Perhaps they were already halfway home. The crowd thinned: he no longer had to stretch. No-one held a placard, with his name or any other. When only officials, police, and baggage-handlers were left he knew he was alone.

At a small kiosk, so dimly lit that at first he thought it closed, he changed his cash for local currency. He thrust into his back pocket the foreign notes, limp and greasy from numberless sweaty hands, and looked for a taxi. Outside, in the grainy darkness beyond the lights of the building, men in voluminous white turbans and white robes like nightshirts flitted like moths, like spectres. Above him were the stars, intense and numerous; he paused for a moment to look up, but after a moment anxiety drove him on. To his great relief, in the taxi queue he found the American.

He said, "No-one came."

The American shrugged with a wry smile, as if to say, What did you expect? They waited together. In front he heard British voices, someone talking about econometrics.

He said, "Excuse me, do you work at the University?" The fellow turned, and before nodding studied his face and clothes. He went on, "I should have been met. No-one came. Where does one stay?"

The fellow looked at him vacantly. "Where you like. We're going to sleep on a friend's roof."

Someone else said, "The University uses the Hotel Percival."

He shared a taxi with the American, who pointed out, under a concrete road bridge, the meeting of the two rivers. He wondered whether his wife and children would enjoy, after all, a holiday here. The American was dropped at the

Grand, a reassuring building with floodlit flags on stainless-steel masts, still full of visible activity despite the hour. The English names: Grand, Percival, were reassuring. After all, the place wasn't that foreign, it was only a few decades after the end of British rule.

The Percival was almost in darkness, occupying half a block. The city-centre blocks were hard-edged and rectilinear. Opposite the hotel, at ground floor level, was a row of galvanised steel shutters in a framework of concrete columns. Inside, the small reception lobby was lit by a yellow bulb and smelt of fenugreek, cigarettes, and hot dusty leather. A porter, small, thin-faced, rather frail, his skin grey rather than black, showed him to the fourth floor. Their slow steps echoed on the *terrazzo*. Each carried two pieces of luggage.

The room was a normal hotel room, if a little severe. A bed, a window, a ceiling fan. On the tiled floor near the window, traces of sand. He pulled back the curtain, exposing a door to a balcony. It faced a concrete building a few yards away. He went out onto it, treading unevenly on more sand, and saw on his right the shuttered building across the street. A car drove by, its headlights dim, the beams a little misty, slowing and beeping at the intersection.

The porter, examining the coin he had been given, left him. He stripped off his shirt, and in the small en-suite splashed cold water over the sweat of his chest and stomach. He ignored his back which, when he lay on the bed, stuck to the sheet. A small black beetle travelled intently across the floor. A fly buzzed in a corner. He watched them with relief: at least it was no worse, these were the only signs of life. Above him the fan beat slowly, the shadows of the blades sliding across the wall in a giant dance. He was here, in a room in Omdurman, scene of the last cavalry charge, a city where gold was wrought.

151

The fan turned with a rhythm which seemed to hesitate. He tried to fit a tune to it. The Prelude to Act One of *Lohengrin* seemed to fit if he increased the tempo, but as it reached its climax, the clash of cymbals, broke away completely. He realised it had never really fitted, that beneath the apparent fluidity of the music, the liquid, molten notes, was a firm unyielding pulse. He tried his own Opus Three. It brought back the smell of the school hall, of the orchestra pit. He thought it would bring back the other woman, grinning at him from over her sewing, but what came was the sight of his children walking towards him in their blazers across the dusty maple flooring. The fan blurred and jumped as his eyes filled with tears. He wiped them and hummed *My Funny Valentine*. That brought back his wife's single bed in her student flat, the pillow with the light fragrance of her hair. He remembered the alien landscape of her body, the giddy sensation when they embraced naked, sweating in the midsummer heat. The fan would not fit *My Funny Valentine*, which came in sallies, in flurries, like the music of *Tristan*, not in a steady thrum-thrum-thrum.

He thought of the money he'd send to his wife, his first pay cheque. Did the University know he existed? His name had not appeared on a white card. But tomorrow he could collect his Initial Payment. Meanwhile the cash he'd changed would last. He was wise not to bring a cheque book or traveller's cheques, so as not to drain the home finances. He wife would just manage till he started to send his pay. With a sudden rush of anxiety he rolled off the narrow bed and reached for his trousers.

He took the dull-textured wad from the back pocket and spread it on the fibre-board bedside table. The rate of exchange was wrong. He'd been cheated. But no, here was the transaction slip, headed in alien script but also in English, the official airport bureau de change. The rate was clearly stated. What he had left, allowing for the taxi fare, was correct. Since he'd first enquired the rate had changed. Or he'd been told wrong. No, it must have changed, the economies of these countries were notoriously unstable. His university salary would convert at a tenth of what he'd believed.

He calculated, with an unsteady heartbeat, the amount he could send home to his wife. It was laughable, hardly worth the commission he'd pay to convert and send it. What would she say?

You who are called my husband, have you yet again deceived me?
— I was led astray.

He stretched on the bed again and watched the fan. He had abandoned any thought of music. It was night. The hotel was quiet. He had no sense of time, his watch was beside the window. He watched the fan turn, just fast enough to blur the edges of the blades, and the edge of the shadow of each blade as it slid across the wall. The beetle crossed the floor, skirting his shoe, the sign of an immense life the beetle could not conceive of. He thought of Wagner, penniless in Paris having quit his dull job in Riga. His failures, exile, loss of Mathilde, impoverished trek from town to town. Then the knock at the door, the fairytale messenger from King Ludwig, the glorious rescue. The fan continued to turn in the breathless hush of the hotel. He heard distant steps in the corridor and listened as they died away. The blades of the fan, the chrome central boss, moved endlessly, with occasional hesitations. Only his reflection in the chrome, greyish-pink on the grey-white bed, was motionless; unbelievably small.

And Gnashing of Teeth

On the wall beside my bed a bright stripe's growing out of nothing. The curtains don't quite meet and the sun's making a thin stick of light across the room. In the light are bits of dust, wool-hairs, pillow-feathers, so many you could spend a year counting, and I've only a few minutes, because it must be nearly time for Daddy to get me up for school.

Far away (I can just hear them) are church bells. In next door's kitchen Mr Driver's coughing: he hasn't gone to work, it's Sunday. Hooray! I can go back to sleep. I can turn to the wall and watch the bright stripe go faint then shine hard again. I can close my eyes and rest because it's light.

Hours ago when the dark was so black I couldn't see the curtains, I woke sweating, feeling the top of my head floating off. I couldn't think. I couldn't breathe. Then miles and miles away I heard a slow motor driving a boat through a huge swamp. The motor was Daddy snoring, chugging Mummy and me towards clear morning water, and I fell asleep again the way I'm falling now …

Ow. That prodding.

"Graham?"

It's Daddy above me with two small faces in his glasses. Behind each face is a striped pillow: mine. Daddy's head has an outline, like the silver one on a Silver Lining chocolate box, but golden. His hair sticks flat and shines. I've tried to brush mine hard with two brushes the way he does, but it doesn't work.

Now he's moved his head and the stripe on the wall's come back. I don't like him to be near this wall because of the messes. One's the torn patch of wallpaper; the other, behind the cupboard, is the one I have to not think about.

He says, "This is a disappointment."

"Disappointment?"

What does he mean? His forehead's rough, not smooth like Mummy's, and folded in a frown.

"Didn't you promise to be up early and light the fire? And meet the milk-cart at the road end for an extra pint?" But he won't let me jump out of bed, he's pushing his legs against it. "Too late now. You'll just have time to eat breakfast and clean your shoes for church."

"Oh heck."

"I beg your pardon?"

I forgot: he hates that expression. He says, "Get up now."

When he stands straight he's so tall his head nearly touches the ceiling. The stripes on his blue Sunday suit go up and up: I don't like that suit, he frightens me in it, watching me dress thinking I'm skinny and weedy and not worth much. I'm looking at his face but my eyes won't meet his. I failed in my duty. In the war Daddy saw a soldier shot for failing in his duty. He showed me a photo of him, smiling with Daddy and other soldiers, all in caps with two buttons on the front. Miss Rhodes says, "That'll wipe the smile off your face," and I know what she means because sometimes, in the early, early morning before it's properly light, I see the soldier's face with the smile wiped off by guns.

When I wake in the dark I always look at the curtains to see if it's many hours till morning. If I can see the pattern I grunt and turn to the wall, glad it can't be long. But I have to keep my eyes shut: if I don't the wallpaper starts to crawl with spiteful witches, monsters, dead people's rotting faces. I picked off a patch of wallpaper near my pillow but it hasn't helped. I see other creatures in the ragged edges of the patch. Now I lie still trying not to look.

Facing the wall's better than facing the room where the melting darkness is deep and alive. Shapeless things—eyes, mouths, teeth, without bodies—come changing and throbbing, at me and away and at me again. Sometimes facing the room I've stayed stiff for hours, not moving, squeezing my eyelids together, thinking hard. Thinking about eternity.

'Compared with eternity one life is less than the splash of a stone in water.' Miss Rhodes made us remember that. Eternity goes on and on, for ever and ever. What would it be like to squeeze my eyelids shut for ever?

Daddy's shaking me. "Don't go back to sleep!"

I put on my clean white shirt and prickly short grey trousers, then pull on my long grey socks, but something's wrong and I feel dizzy. Daddy's straightening the bedclothes and he's noticed the wallpaper. My skin's gone cold. His finger's bony, with black hairs and thick knuckles, and he's making it follow the edge of the tear.

"Did you do this?" he asks, looking into my face.

"Well, sort of."

"Sort of. What does that mean?"

"It was sort of an accident."

"I see. And how did this 'accident' occur?"

I can't find an answer. It's like when it's getting later and later before school and I can't find my cap. Daddy looks very interested, like Mrs Driver's cat looking at birds. One day I'll grow a moustache like his and not be so frightened of him. I wish this was just a bad dream.

I tell him, "I had a nightmare."

He repeats, "A nightmare," showing his teeth like he does

when he bites a penny. I wish I hadn't said it. When I used to have nightmares about huge webs and sinking sand, Mummy would come when I cried out and soothe me to sleep. Now I'm at school Daddy makes fun of my crying out and asks, "Don't you want to grow up?" Of course I do. Maybe I can explain like a grown-up.

"I dreamed this tiger came and I said, 'Go away, go away,' doing my hand like this, and when I woke up the wall was all sort of scratched."

He takes off his glasses and rubs his nose. I don't like the way his eyelids are wrinkled. His eyes are grey like rainclouds and sunk into his head. They look sad. I feel sad too. I thought the tiger dream would make him understand, but it hasn't. It happened a long time ago. Now the same bad dream keeps coming. I'm always in the same place, standing on a moor in half dark or maybe mist, the land sloping to the left. There's always coarse grass I can hardly see, fuzzy clumps of heather, everything fading into speckled nothing. I hear sheep crying and look for them hard, but I never see them.

Daddy puts his glasses back on. "This was deliberate. You used some implement."

If I ask what an implement is he'll say I'm changing the subject. I tell him, "I saw faces in the pattern." I wish my voice didn't come so shaky. The skin between his eyebrows has gone into folds: the pores are like little strawberry seeds.

"This was wilful destruction." Saying 'wilful' he wrinkles his nose and shows his teeth: it must mean something horrible. I try to look at his face but my eyes still slide away. How long is he going to stand there quiet?

He says, "A little liar."

Now he's clumping downstairs and I feel dried up inside. Why couldn't I really explain? If I hadn't started with the tiger he might have believed the faces. Why couldn't I tell him about the moor?

I don't want any breakfast now. I'm not going to look up from this plate. I'll just eat my bacon and count the pink roses round the edge, then the thorns on the twisty stems. There's the telephone. Daddy's gone to answer it.

Mummy says, "No use looking at me. Your father's very disappointed in you. Says you told him lies."

She looks away into the hall, listening to what Daddy's saying, her head on one side, pulling a lock of her curly hair. Daddy's voice sounds deep and Sundayish. I think he's telling the church people what I've done.

Mummy looks at me again. "I wash my hands of the whole affair." She drinks her tea, looking into the distance. This bacon's got little round bones. It doesn't seem like part of a pig. Where does the blood go?

In the hall Daddy says, "Ah yes, Matthew Chapter Eight."

I ask Mummy, "Is that about 'love your enemies'?"

She can see Daddy through the open door. She looks at him quickly, then at me. "Is what?"

"Matthew Chapter Eight."

She's looking into the distance again. "It could be. I've no idea."

"Love your enemies, love your enemies." (They said that at the Victory Thanksgiving service.)

"Be quiet, Graham."

I ask, "Does Daddy love his enemies?"

She looks right at me. I must remember her face to crayon at school. Her eyes are the easiest: I can use the crayon for the sky. She says, "Pardon?" so I ask again. She screws up her lips. "I'm sure he tries."

"Even the Germans?"

Daddy's moved and now I can see a bit of him. His head's

bent over the telephone the way he bends it to pray. I can't see his face but I think he's looking at Mummy because she's flicking her eyes towards him, tugging her hair.

I say, a bit louder, "Even Hitler?"

She looks cross and squirmy. Why can't she talk to me? She and Daddy hardly ever talk at the table, and all the chewing and swallowing, the knives and plates clicking and ringing, make *me* feel cross and squirmy.

"Well?"

"That's a very difficult question, Graham."

"All right, tell me why Hitler killed the Jews and why the Jews killed Jesus."

"Graham ..."

"And will they all be punished? Will they all go to hell?"

Mummy jumps up with a little gasp and puts the cereal packets away. The phone goes ping and now she's talking to Daddy, trying to keep her voice quiet. She says, "He's asking ..." then I can't hear, then, "You'll have to ..." The door's pulled shut. What are they saying? I'd better drink my tea.

Now it's time to go and I'm alone with Daddy in the hall, waiting for him to say something, or explode. But he just keeps his lips pressed together and shoves me a bit helping me on with my coat. The hall smells of damp coats, cooking polish, and Daddy's shaving cream. I feel I'm three again, when he used to lift me and press my face against his. I look up to see if he remembers, but he's looking somewhere else.

The road to church is downhill: coming back you don't mind walking uphill because you're thinking about dinner. Daddy's met a man he knows and they're ahead. I'm with Mummy. Who's she talking to, me or herself?

"They really should cut that tree back. Oh, a magpie, how

splendid! There's a notice in Ramsden's window. Can you read it, Graham? 'Under new Management'." She makes a tutting noise. "Looks as if Jews have bought it."

She must mean the boy beside that car, and the man trying to unlock the shop door. How does she know they're Jews? The car's a Morris Oxford: it can't be a Jewish car because Mr McDonald's got one. The man looks cross but the boy's just whistling, hands in his pockets. Doesn't he know he's going to be punished for killing Jesus? I'll ask Mummy to get him to come to church to ask forgiveness. Or maybe I won't. She might go squirmy again.

I forgot you can ask God to forgive you. Now I'm skipping along in the sunshine. Better not let Daddy see me. The tops of the garden walls must be hot: if I didn't have to walk on the outside I'd run my hand along. Each leaf in the privet hedges stands out; each lamp post makes a stripe of shadow; each flagstone winks with shiny stuff. In church I'll ask God to forgive the lie and the wallpaper, and afterwards ask Daddy the same.

Here we are. This old man handing out hymnbooks looks fierce in his old-fashioned collar. He doesn't seem to want to give me one. When he does it's cold, heavy, dark shiny brown. These thick doors are dark brown too, and the black hooks holding them back are like claws.

Inside it's chilly and smells holy. The organ doesn't sound cheerful like Sandy McPherson's on the wireless, just sort of worried. The window tops point to heaven, Miss Rhodes says. If I wanted to rise to heaven I'd be stopped by all those planks and beams. Behind the pulpit is the hymn board: 46, 187 and so on. There's a fly on the 7. Suppose it set off to walk round the walls till it came back to the board, then set off again. Even if it went round and back a million billion times it wouldn't use up eternity.

Why's Daddy got up and gone to the front in the middle of this hymn? Is he going to tell everyone what I've done? Oh, he's going to that table thing, the lectern I think it's called, and he's opening the big Bible to read from.

Now we've sat down and Daddy's reading, but it doesn't sound like him. He keeps stopping and starting in a posh chanting voice like the minister's. His shiny hair with its dead straight parting goes bigger then smaller as he looks down at the page then up again. Everyone's listening to what God wrote. I don't understand it but I'm glad it's my father reading. His face is like a soldier's at attention because God's like a field-marshal only higher. Maybe if he was told 'at ease' he'd stop looking stern and smile because he's proud to be reading.

While we're eating our roast beef I'll tell him I'm very, very sorry about the wallpaper. I'll help him to patch it like those workmen at school. They cut the edges straight with a knife and scraped off the spoilt part. They grumbled about using bits of old roll because of austerity. Daddy and I can grumble the same way as we pull the bed away from the wall, the bed and —

The cupboard! Oh no, no, I'd forgotten about the cupboard. Now we've got to stand for another hymn; my legs are shaking and my stomach doesn't feel as if it's there. He doesn't know about the ink behind the cupboard. If there was a piece of wood on the back the ink bottle wouldn't have slid. It isn't a proper cupboard, just a small painted box with a door and a flat top to write on. It was a horrible thing to happen at New Year when I was filling my pen to start my new diary. I don't know what the stain's like. Each time the thought of it comes I push it back into the dark inside my head.

We'll drag back the cupboard and there'll be a long hush.

There it'll be: the stain, like a giant spider, a witch's hand. What will I say? How can I say I'm sorry now? The minister's going into the pulpit looking serious, looking over his glasses with sharp eyes. That white V upside down instead of a tie is bands. It never gets dirty because he never does any sins. He's the only one allowed to step up there closer to God.

He looks down, then up, and says, "My text is Matthew Eight, verse twelve: 'But the children of the kingdom shall be cast out into outer darkness: there shall be weeping and gnashing of teeth.'"

He goes on, in that voice that makes me sleepy, but I feel wide awake now wondering what he said. I wish he'd stop talking so I can remember. I'll have to wait till he says his text again.

"But the children of the kingdom shall be cast out into outer darkness."

I hoped I'd heard it wrong.

"Now, what does Jesus mean by outer darkness?" He asks the way grown-ups do when they know the answer. I know the answer too. He means the middle of the night when it's black and still, and your blood swishes louder and louder till the noise fills the room, and you cling to the bed like a sailor to a raft, hoping for morning. Except that in outer darkness there's no bed, no morning, nothing. Nothing at all.

I wish I was wrong. I wish it didn't mean that. He's explaining, but with words I don't understand.

Daddy's at the end of the pew. He understands. I wish I could ask him afterwards, "Who deserves to be cast out? Does it mean *all* the children? Is outer darkness dark all over, or can you see, faint and far away, the light of God and the angels?"

He's noticed me staring and looks very cross. I look down. Those cracks in the floor are like tiny rivers; that broken match is covered in dust; that flake of hymnbook back is held together by the cloth. If I look and look these things might not go away. Please, God, don't put the dark instead of them yet.

There's Mummy's shoe, smooth and grey with bits cut out over the toes, very different from mine. If I ask Mummy she'll get worried and keep looking at Daddy. If I bang my head or cut myself she'll comfort me, but she's washed her hands of anything to do with lies and sin. Daddy has to deal with those. And I can't ask him because of my secret, the stain on the wall in black permanent ink.

Cast into outer darkness. It'll be a hundred times worse than the empty moor. There won't be grass or the sound of sheep. First God's voice will thunder, then red eyes will glare while scaly hands push me away. I'll rush into nothing. I'll see horrible faces on skeleton bodies, faces without lips or eyes, like the ones I looked at for hours in that picture magazine before Mummy snatched it away. Then even those will go, and I'll be alone.

Everyone's chatting in little groups around the church entrance. Mummy and Daddy are talking to an old lady about her dog. The sun's so bright people are shading their eyes.

I'm on my own in shadow. I like the sun but I can't enjoy it now it's going to be taken away. I close my eyes to try the dark and grind my teeth together. Is that gnashing? I'm not sure, but there'll be time to find out.

The Smell of Happiness

At the top of the cellar steps, above the door, was the shelf where Arthur kept the jar. Looking up into the dark he'd wait for his eyes to adjust. Then, in the angle where plaster met brown boards, he'd see it. Safely wedged between linseed oil and metal primer, corded with grimy cobwebs.

Sometimes he took it down. The handwriting on the label was so faded he could hardly read it. The jar was from a lab, clear glass, the bakelite top covered by brown paper ingrained with dust. He'd wipe the jar on his sleeve and hold it to the light. It looked empty. Arthur knew it was not.

He tried to inspect it when Vera was reading or sewing. But sometimes the door from the front room opened and he heard her stick, her irregular step.

She said, "Doing a spot of painting?"

They looked at each other with faint smiles.

"Just checking."

"I'm checking on you. You shouldn't reach. Don't want to find you dead on the cellar steps."

But it was her he found dead. In January, the early hours of a Sunday. He'd asked whether she was coming to bed.

"You go up, I'll just finish this."

He woke at three, anxious not finding her beside him. She was still where he'd left her. He took the sewing needle from between her icy fingers.

After the funeral, when the children, grandchildren, and friends went back to their normal lives, and he was left to deal with his new one, he put the jar on the kitchen windowsill. It would drive home, while he washed up, the fact that things were different. That when he saw youths in baseball caps leap over a neighbour's wall, he couldn't ask Vera's advice. That when he thought of a plan to save money he needn't go halfway along the hall before turning back. The jar looked strange dusted and fully lit. It unnerved him that the red line edging the label was still clear. That the glass reflected the cacti on either side.

When the cacti collapsed like leaky balloons he threw them out. It had been Vera who watered them, forbidding him in case they got sodden. He couldn't break the habit of keeping his hands off. Without the reflections the jar looked forlorn. He wanted to cry, looking at it. The sight of the windowsill with jar and cacti had already become familiar. It shocked him how long it had been like that. It was summer already. He wiped the sill clean and left it empty. The jar he put in a drawer behind his socks.

It was a year before he looked at it. He'd tried to be busy, joining clubs, visiting the children, even seeing his estranged brother in Wales. The anniversary of Vera's death didn't disturb him. In January it was a struggle just to keep going, to feed himself, and he slept a lot. It was the anniversary of throwing out the cacti that shook him. He couldn't sleep. Sometimes the nights were hot, and the noise of aircraft, of groups of youths and girls shouting after closing time, pressed in through the open window. On the TV news there were pictures of dying children. Someone urinated through the letterbox. Then there was heavy rain, drumming on the skylight over the stairs, leaving a brown stain on the bedroom ceiling.

He huddled in the bed that seemed incredibly wide. He stared at the wall, the chest of drawers. The light from a streetlamp laid a bright strip across the sock drawer. It was a sign. Now must be the time to open the jar.

The day he met Vera his boots were falling apart. He was out with the local rambling club, and although it was a fine spring day he regretted coming. The blue and white mottled sky, the clear rugged lines of gritstone edges, didn't cure his vexation. Through the worn soles he felt every stone, and whenever the group forded a shallow beck his socks took up more water. He'd ordered new boots weeks ago, and to his disgust they still hadn't come. Also, his left hand was bandaged from the acid burn at work. It throbbed, but the chief technician's comment bothered him more.

"Good thing it was just your hand, eh? That it didn't ruin that film-star profile."

He knew he wasn't good looking: face too thin, nose and ears too big. If he asked a girl for a dance there was always that telltale moment before she said brightly, "Oh, all right."

When the group rested he sat alone with his lunch-box, grimly studying the long horizon. This walk was pointless, like the route marches in the Air Force, when all he'd wanted was to be in the hut varnishing propeller-blades. Someone came over and sat on a rock beside him. A girl with a big mouth, wearing a Fair Isle jumper. He ignored her.

She said, "Hold this, could you?"

The strap of her canvas rucksack had come unstitched. Someone had to take the weight and steady it while she sewed it. She worked away, now and then giving it a tug. Arthur tugged back as a joke, cautiously at first. It became a game between them.

He said, "You're efficient."

She looked at him, not sure what he meant, and when he

met her gaze he felt he'd been picked up and shaken. After a long pause he said, "I mean, carrying needle and thread."

"I like to keep things together."

She asked what happened to his hand, and Arthur even dared to include what the chief technician said. She laughed. Her mouth was definitely too big.

She said, "He's envious. He'd rather be you." And added, her mouth suddenly small and prim, "Sarcasm's the lowest form of wit."

The rest of the walk they couldn't stop thinking of things to say. When the party got off the bus they stood for a moment, then both spoke.

"Would you like to—"

"Do you ever—"

He said, "I was going to ask you to the pictures."

And she: "I was asking if you ever go roller-skating."

His new boots didn't arrive for another fortnight. He collected them on a Saturday. The evening before, for the first time, he'd kissed Vera. First on the neck, among the wisps of loose brown hair, then on the lips. He couldn't believe how soft her mouth was.

He took the boots out of the box and tore away the tissue. He felt so full he might explode. He put them on, laced them, strode up and down. It was like walking on clouds. They were exactly right. It was fate. He'd saved for months, hardly going out, having a thin time. Now they were paid for. He thought, And there's Vera. Even at work—especially at work—he'd stop, finger frozen on a pipette or among his notes, thinking, And there's Vera.

The boots had an unusual smell. A broad, fresh, expansive smell, no doubt from the tanning. It had nothing to do with his life so far, with the engine oil and aircraft dope of the Air

Force, the chemicals in the lab, the sphagnum moss of the moors. It made him think of unknown farms, with dogs and horses and hay, of distant forests of oak or pine, of deep river-pools full of trout. Words like hide, resin, saddle-soap, failed to come near. It was simply the smell of happiness.

There were the boots, and there was Vera. His life was full. He knew it wouldn't last, that this was a peak he'd have to come down from. He wrapped the boots, and on Monday took them to work. He stood them in an old fume-cupboard, seldom used, and beside them a clear glass jar. Over boots and jar he inverted a cardboard box lined with waxed paper. He closed the cupboard, hoping the chief technician wouldn't press his nose to the glass. He didn't.

Arthur removed the boots on Friday, very early. It was the ideal day: the lab surrounded him like a palm-house, full of planes of bright glass. The chemicals in their jars were the colours of birds of paradise. The evening before, he and Vera had confessed that they were in love. He couldn't believe it. All week he'd been sure something would go wrong, that they'd lose each other. They didn't. It was only well after they married that small betrayals and resentments gathered, and they went through times of coldness and isolation.

Now he set aside the box and quickly screwed the lid on the jar. The smell of the boots had concentrated under the box. Already it took him back to the time when he first kissed Vera, made his heart race with the danger, fear of rejection, crossing the line from ordinary friendship, dizzy surrender to fate.

He tightened the lid till the rubber seal squeaked, then hurried to the bench, and inverting the jar, plunged the top into molten wax. One eye on the clock in case the chief technician appeared, he dipped repeatedly, letting each coating harden. When he was satisfied he taped brown paper over to protect the wax. He stuck on a blank label and wondered what to write. *Boots*. But this wasn't really about boots. *Vera*. But over the years (if there were to be years) the pleasure of saying her name would give way to habit. In the end he just wrote the year, forty-eight.

When they got engaged he showed her the jar.

Vera said, "What are you trying to hold on to?"

"Happiness."

She laughed. "And can you?"

"The memory of it, yes."

She said, "Eh, it's a strange man I'm marrying."

Now, a year and a half after her death, he felt at the back of the drawer. There was the jar, round and still; the glass cold, inscrutable. Behind it the air of forty-six years ago. The smell of the boots that opened up on Crib Goch and ended in a Welsh dustbin. Long since replaced. He knew he'd have to be quick, breathe in the precious fumes before they diffused. Perhaps if he closed it after a second he'd get another taste, but that would be all. The smell of happiness, magic carpet to forty-eight, would be lost.

The thought made him cry. He sank his head in the pillow and sobbed as he hadn't done since Vera's death. He thought of things she'd said. 'I like to keep things together.' He wished he'd remembered more, written them down, because now there were no new ones, just heavy silence. The tears left him drained, purified. He'd open the jar when his need was greater.

A few months later, after picking up his pension, he walked as usual down a path between gable ends. Three youths in baseball caps ran at him. He might have seen them before, he couldn't tell. Not satisfied with his money they pushed him to his knees, and with their knees battered his chest. He thought he was dying. Perhaps he'd see Vera again, perhaps not. The chaplain who called in intensive care didn't seem sure either. He was more concerned for Arthur to forgive his attackers. Arthur couldn't deal with such meaningless ill-will. He got through the time in hospital by thinking about the jar.

The house felt bleak. It smelt of stale sink-water. When his children finished sorting him out and left he went to the drawer. The jar was there, no-one had stolen it. He sat at the table and picked at the sticky tape with trembling fingers. He loosened a corner and pulled, but instead of peeling it flaked, brittle with age. He tried again, more urgently; impatient, now the years of waiting were over, to revive his withered memory. The jar slipped from his grasp and rolled across the table. He grabbed at it and pain grasped him by the ribs. Gasping, he caught the jar one-handed right on the edge. It was a while before he could bring his other hand round to secure it.

He learned from that. Why open the jar when desperate? Better when calm, waking perhaps from a peaceful dream. And not now, in autumn, when the sun didn't clear the roofs till ten, or stayed a mysterious bright patch on the clouds. He locked the jar away. When the laburnums were hung with warm yellow he took it out. He placed it ready on the bedside table, on what had been Vera's side. He gathered implements, a penknife, a tool for opening jars.

The thought of the opening made his heart unsteady. Sometimes, in anticipation, he tried to remember that marvellous week, the journey from awkward loneliness to excitement, hope, to knowing he was loved. All he could bring to mind were tired images from photos. One of Vera opening a Thermos, her face in shadow. Another at a dance, her shoulders very white, frowning against the flash.

One morning he woke late. Outside, a wood pigeon repeated its ridiculous call. He kept his eyes shut, convinced that he heard Vera breathing beside him. He wanted to reach out, but feared she might disappear. If he kept still in the hot bed she might hook her bare thigh over his, rub her face against his shoulder. The feeling faded. He opened his eyes and saw the jar. If there was a time to open it, it was now.

Ignoring the tape he cut through the brown paper. The wax was intact, a little darker than on the morning in the empty lab. It would all be there, the smell of the new boots, the memory of youth and happiness, the sense of an endless future. He dug his fingernails into the wax—and stopped.

This *was* the future. He'd remember the new boots, but could he forget throwing them away? He'd feel the joy of thinking: And there's Vera, but also their anger with one another over misspent money, his attitude to the children, her always wanting to move house. He'd remember their first long walks, but also Vera's failed hip, the walking stick still there in the wardrobe. With the flat of the knife he smoothed the wax.

Over the years the wax darkened more. The cut edges of the brown paper flaked and split. The label faded, and he forgot the year it had recorded. Some summers, in early morning, the glass reflected a bright square of curtain. Some winter mornings he thought there was something in there, but wiping off the condensation he saw the jar was empty. The air inside was as clear as ever.

Acknowledgments

Grateful acknowledgment is made to all the editors of publications or programmes in which these stories first appeared or were broadcast:

The Affectionate Punch: 'Doing It'
BBC Radio 4 Morning Story: 'The Visitor', 'The Smell of Happiness'
Bridport Prize Anthology: 'The Fan'
Iron: 'And Gnashing of Teeth'
New Welsh Reader: 'Theory and Design in the Age of Innocence'
Paris Transcontinental: 'Snaps'
Scribble (USA): 'Creels'
Soundwaves (Federation of Writers Scotland anthology): 'Worthy'
Stand: 'Romey and Jullit', 'Trouble'
Staple: 'Whole'
Willesden Herald New Short Stories 5: 'Homecoming'

'Whiskey and Halva' won first prize in the Doolin Writers competition.
'My Life With Eva' was shortlisted in the Ilkley Literature Festival Competition.
'Worthy' won third prize in the Federation of Writers Scotland short story competition.
'Doing It' was performed as a monologue by Loose

Exchange Theatre Company at the Soho Poly Theatre as part of *Improbabilities*.

Thanks also to John Ashbrook, Elizabeth Baines, James Barr, Ann Byrne-Sutton, Deborah Freeman, Christine Harrison, Helen O'Leary, Ann Stephens, and Peter Oram, and especially my wife Rosemarie, for interesting discussions and useful comments on my work over the years. And thanks to Ilona David for the excellent cover painting. Special thanks also to Richard Davies and Carly Holmes at Parthian.